I0671243

AWAKENING
THE CANNON FODDER
SERIES BOOK 1

Andrew C. Suhrer

AWAKENING

ISBN: 0692490418

ISBN-13: 978-0692490419

Awakening - The Cannon Fodder Series Book 1

Cover Design: David London of London Studios
Edited by: Dequiana Jackson of Inspired Marketing, Inc.

This is a work of fiction. Names, characters, places and incidents are either the product of the author's imagination or are used fictitiously, and any resemblance to actual persons, living or dead, business establishments, events or locales is entirely coincidental.

PROLOGUE

A rubber glove forced a set of eyelids apart, letting in the surrounding light. It felt like a burning needle being poked in the man's retinas. He grunted as he tried to close his eyes and move at the same time. Immediately, a happy voice exclaimed, "Patient is responsive to outside stimuli. I was wondering when I would get a reaction out of you."

The patient snapped back at him, "I'll give you an even greater reaction if you don't stop touching my eyes!"

"I see your communication skills are still intact. Now whether or not you can follow through on threats..." the apparent doctor responded as he released the restraints on the patient's limbs. Quickly the man sat up, but the doctor put his hand on the patient's forehead, stopping him. He moved a monitor out of the way telling the man, "You wouldn't want to bump your head again, might forget something important. Speaking of memory loss, what is the last thing you remember?"

"Well..." He thought about it, but nothing came to mind. In fact, everything in his mind was a blur. The patient looked around hoping to get his bearings. He saw several other cylinder shaped beds, medical equipment, red hazmat suits, monitors showing all the vital signs of his body and white ambient lighting. The room was surprisingly cramped, which didn't help."

"Oh crap!" He felt a sudden tug from his belly as a cord was yanked out. As the gray haired doctor with dark skin and a white lab coat cleaned off the cord, he sighed, "You don't say. Do you know where you are?"

The patient looked around, started to panic, and tried to remember anything from before this moment. He guessed, "I'm in some sort of ship's infirmary?"

"You still have deduction skills. We could make use of you yet," the doctor told him as he tapped away on a holographic data pad. The patient took another look around and caught his reflection in the mirror. He saw that he was wearing green coveralls, a brown t-shirt, a tan utility belt, and black boots. The patient saw his face, and it felt like he was seeing a stranger. His face was shaved. His skin looked like it had been burned. His eyes were dark and artificial looking, and his brown hair was cut short. He looked back over at the doctor and asked, "Who are you?"

The doctor smiled, "Funny, a man who can't remember who he is asking for others' identities. Don't feel too bad. I don't even remember my name."

The patient's eyebrows went up, "Really?"

He laughed, "I see you have a hard time with sarcasm. You'll learn. I just like going by Doc. Now, please stand up."

The man got off the bed, and it folded up behind him against the bulkhead. He looked down at his hands and saw they didn't have any veins sticking out. He couldn't help but have a feeling that most of his body parts were artificial. Information started to stream before his eyes in a flash, startling him. "Relax," Doc said, "Just the implants kicking in."

"Implants?" The patient then saw the cut marks and felt numb all over. "That's not all," Doc responded. He explained that the patient's feelings were right. Most of his body was now artificial. His breathing was even being simulated by fake lungs. In a slight panic, the patient checked his groin. To his relief, that was at least real. He asked, "What did you do to me?"

Doc walked around the patient testing his limbs and tapping away at his holo-monitor, "Saving lives, preventing further injury and minimizing infection in the most effective way I can."

As Doc continued checking his vital signs, the patient got frustrated, "Would you stop being so coy, and just give me a straight answer! What happened to my body?"

"Be careful of what you ask; you might not like the answers," said a deep voice from behind them. The patient turned around and saw what could only be described as an alien. He was taller than a normal man, had four thick red eyes, a round pumpkin like head, a wide smile with shark like teeth, elongated limbs with large hands and feet, two slots for a nose, slicked back hair that looked like bug legs on top of his head, glimmering dark green scales that covered his skin, and a small, oval shaped torso. He had on a dark armored suit that only added to his already intimidating sight. "What the hell?"

The alien walked toward the patient with a relaxed stroll, "You're not in the afterlife just yet. You've actually been given a second chance, old friend, maybe even a clean slate. But it's going to get tarnished very quickly if you don't deliver. There's one last test I want to run to see if you're worth our efforts."

The patient stepped back looking around rapidly, "What? Another test? Really?!"

He brought a cigar to his mouth as he calmly told the patient, "There's going to be three people coming in to kill you. Kill them first, and if you survive, we'll talk. The test starts now."

Doc and the alien both stepped back as the patient

heard a door opening. The lights shut off, and the patient was again blind. His blindness only lasted for a moment. His eyes switched to night vision, and he saw a woman coming toward him with two, hot glowing knives. He dodged her first lunge with ease. She came back with a swipe that just barely missed his face. He felt the heat from the blades, but he wasn't sweating or breathing hard. The patient stayed on the balls of his feet and moved backward as the woman kept trying to stab him. She made a swipe for his head again. Instinctively, he leaned back, reached up and grabbed her arm. The patient rotated forward snapping the woman's arm and then hit it with full force, breaking it. As she cried, he grabbed the knife and stabbed her in the throat. One down, two to go.

There was a red flash in his eyes and, without thinking, he turned around, keeping the dead woman in front of him as a shield. There was a loud tapping sound as a plasma round impacted his human shield. The patient pushed the dead body away, keeping the knife, and bolted forward. The person fired his pistol three more times with each shot missing its mark. The patient leaped forward and rolled towards him as he kept firing. He ended up right in front of the shooter and thrust the knife into his heart before he could get off his next shot. The man dropped the pistol and let out a grunt before his eyes rolled into the back of his head. Two down.

Before the man could hit the floor, the patient felt a hand grab his shoulder and spin him around violently. His next attacker was in an armored suit. He punched the patient in the face as he went for the knife. The patient fell backward onto the ground as another punch hit him in the head. He felt it, but it wasn't too painful. It was just enough to get him focused. The patient reached over, grabbed the pistol from the floor and shot him. There was a flash of light as the round impacted some type of energy shield.

The man went for the pistol and both struggled against each other to control the weapon. The patient was losing his power, but he still had his speed. The man let the pistol go and quickly went back for the knife. The patient pried it from his hand while dodging a plasma round that zoomed past his head. He jabbed the blade into the armored man's wrist, grabbed the pistol and repeatedly shot him in the head. The armor got weaker with every hit taken. The pistol ran out of rounds, so the patient started to hit him over the head with it. The blow was hard enough to rip off part of the armor. With his other hand, the patient stabbed downward into the opening, stabbing the man in his neck. With the three attackers now dead, the patient hoped the testing period was finally over.

The lights suddenly came back on, and the patient saw his last victim's eyes. They were wide open in their final moments of pain. The patient backed up, letting the dead man drop to the deck with steam still rising from his wounds. He heard the alien clapping his hands together, "Good! You are worth a second chance after all!"

Doc and several nurses walked in. Silently, they hauled the dead bodies away and cleaned up the mess the patient had made. The alien motioned for the items the patient held. Reluctantly, he relinquished the pistol and knife while the alien's cigar smoke blew in his face. "What was that all about?" the patient asked.

"Needed to see if you could still perform. A killer who can't fight is useless to me. If you want to find out who you are, you must be able to fight." The alien leaned back on the bulkhead, dropping ashes on the deck, "Revenge will be ours, Alec Dumont."

"Alec? That's my name?" Alec asked, his back straight with his full attention on the alien. "It's the one I gave you. I'm called Yosemite."

Alec gave a confused look, "Yosemite? Who gave you that name, and what are you exactly?"

He smiled, "The name of my race is unable to be said in your primitive language. The best word I can think of when addressing my species is Stallions. My real name is also beyond your primitive tongue. As for the name Yosemite, what's wrong what that?"

"Nothing. It's fine," Alec said as he fought back the urge to chuckle. Yosemite leaned forward, "Now to cut to the chase, I need you to kill people. Before you ended up in a coma, Doc saved what he could, so you might remember some things."

"Only some things? What happened to me? Did I get really drunk last night or something?" Alec asked trying to guess what was going on. Yosemite got a kick out of it, "Close analogy."

"Okay, so I'm some sort of agent that works for you. My body has been upgraded with technology, and I'm guessing I'm on a star ship. I'm also going to be killing people for you. Am I missing something?" Alec stated while trying to put together the pieces of his current mission. Yosemite responded, "Yes, yes, yes, the Pandora ship, yes, and yes."

"How's more violence going to help?" Alec wondered out loud. Yosemite laughed, "Violence is never the question. It's the answer! So are you ready to die for a pointless cause?"

Alec looked at him for a second wondering if he was all there. He went on, "Die? No. Kill? Apparently so. You said I was missing something. What?"

Yosemite dropped his cigar and lifted his four eyebrows, "A lot."

He came forward so quickly that Alec couldn't react in time. The alien grabbed Alec's head and yanked it backwards. Yosemite then held a vial of a glowing liquid over him and forced it into his eye. Alec gasped as he saw several flashing images that became clearer the faster they flashed. It was like watching an old film projector start up. This must have been one of the memories Doc spoke of. Slowly, everything came into view.

CHAPTER 1
2189
AWAKENING
TIME UNKNOWN
LOCATION UNKNOWN

ALEC was face down in front of a toilet and gasping for air in between dry heaves. A woman yelled his name, "Alec!"

"Almost there," he replied as he cringed. Slowly he stood up, "All done."

Alec walked out of the women's restroom blocking his head as the woman hit him repeatedly with her purse and yelled, "You idiot! Couldn't you read between the lines?!"

"I thought I did. There's a woman named 'Sparkles' who can show us a good time. Her number is," Before he could finish, the woman slapped him across the face. "That was graffiti! Idiot!"

"Looked like an invitation to me," he laughed as she slapped him again. Alec asked, "Why can't we have fun like that anymore?" as he took a hit in the groin and fell to the ground. The woman picked him back up, "Okay. Now I've had my fun, too. Let's go."

"Come on. The night is still young," he protested as she pulled him along. The woman guided him quickly through the bar's exit where his eyes were met with the blinding light of the sun. The woman snapped, "Night, my ass. It's fucking noon!"

"That's bullshit! Where did the time go?" Alec asked as he held his eyes. They walked out to a balcony that overlooked a massive forest. "I think it went into the toilet along with whatever self-respect you had left."

"Alisa, don't be a downer," he laughed as almost tripped over his own feet. Alisa caught him and kept him walking along the path. "You've had enough booze and pills to be rock bottom without my help."

They continued along on what looked like a city skyscraper in the middle of forest on a sunny day. They made their way to a vertical bus that traveled up and down the skyscraper. "Try not to throw up in here," Alisa told him.

"Trying and doing are two different things," Alec replied, still nursing his hangover. He took a seat against the window as the bus ascended into the air, taking them up several stories in a matter of seconds. Alec was moving so sluggishly that Alisa had to pull him off the bus in order to get off at the right stop. He was nearly passed out in her arms as she dragged him back to his apartment. She knocked on the door, and their roommate Duncan McCormick answered, "Again?"

"Really that surprised, Duncan?" Alisa asked him sarcastically as he helped her drag Alec inside. They laid him on the couch, and Alisa sat down next to him with a sigh. Duncan got a cup of coffee for each of them and handed Alec his cup with a warning, "Don't drink it too fast. You'll get sick."

Alec laughed, "I'm already sick."

Duncan asked, "Are you talking about the alcoholism, your mind or that infection you told me about?"

Alisa immediately stood up, "Infection?"

"Nothing to worry about, Alisa. I got that fixed," he answered. Alec tried to put his cup on the end table next to the couch but missed. Coffee splattered across the floor, and Duncan snapped, "You pain in the ass! I just got this place clean from the last time you messed it up!"

"It took you that long? You make a bad maid," Alec said sleepily as he laid back down on the verge of passing out again. "No you don't!"

Duncan walked over and punched him in the

stomach. Alec groaned, "Really?"

"Yes, really. You do know that you have class in two hours, right?" Duncan pointed out. Alec rolled to his side, "Fuck school. The government is paying for it. It's my turn to screw them over for a change!"

"You bent over and gave them the opportunity. Now Alisa, did you really think it was a good idea to take him out and get drunk last night?" Duncan asked getting more annoyed with them by the second." Alisa answered, "He was drunk when I bumped into him. I tried helping, but he couldn't rise to the occasion, if you know what I mean."

"Wait! You were just using me?" Alec pointed at her. Alisa got up and went for the door, "You're all used up now, Alec. I don't know if I'll see you again, and I don't care. Thanks for the coffee, Duncan."

Alisa walked out leaving them alone. Alec rolled back over, "Why does everyone use me?"

"We've had this conversation before. She's right. You're used up. I'm tired of this shit." Duncan started walking way, and Alec screamed, "You're walking out on me, too?"

"No, you're going to be doing to walking. I'm kicking you out as soon as you're sober," Duncan told him. Alec tried standing up but fell right back down, "What?

Duncan, wait. Don't you think you're being rash?"

"If I was being rash I would kick you out right now. I'll give you until your hangover is over. After that, I want you out of here!" Duncan barked at him. The gravity of the situation sobered Alec up a little bit, "Come on! I looked out for you while we worked together. Hell, I jumped on several mechanical grenades for you! Doesn't that count for something?"

"Like I said, that's why I'm giving you until the booze is out of your system before I send you on your way. I tried to help you. I wanted to help you, but you just couldn't keep it together. I'm tired of cleaning up after your messes, and I'm tired of you complaining about how the military didn't live up to your expectations. At some point we all have to grow up and realize that the fiction we see on the screens isn't how it plays out in real life. Real people have responsibilities."

"You can…," Alec stopped himself mid-sentence. "I'm sorry, for what it's worth."

"So am I, Alec. You should try hanging with the homeless vets. They live in the agrarian levels. Get some rest. You'll need it." With that, Duncan walked out of the living room and left Alec alone. He leaned back on the couch and stared out the window at the flashing images of nature moving in front of him. Realizing he just got kicked out of another apartment, Alec muttered quietly, "Crap."

"Take a seat, Dumont," the history professor told Alec as he prepared to leave. Class was out, but Alec was told to stay afterwards. He fell back down into the seat and looked up at the lights in dismay. The holo-projector flashed 'Mars University' as the professor commented, "Surprised you even showed up. What happened this time?"

Alec sighed, "Same shit, different day, Professor Victor."

Victor rolled his eyes, "Pushing people away, burning bridges, and getting the boot again? McCormick held out hope for you longer than most did."

"Close enough, and yeah, he did." He leaned forward holding his head as Professor Victor shook his side to side. "So why did you choose to take this history class, Mr. Dumont? Can't really get a good job on the outside with a degree in this field."

"If no one gives a shit about what happened in the past, then it's doomed to repeat itself," he told him. The professor pointed to the holo-screen above him and asked,

"Kind of like the micro wars of the twentieth and twenty first century?"

"Yeah. Hard to believe the Western and Eastern powers of ancient Earth managed to keep the conflict going that long. Shouldn't the Eastern power have fallen apart because of bad economics?"

"If you were on time to my class, you would have learned that the East should have collapsed in the late 1980s or even as late as the 90s. Instead, the West actually bailed out the East long enough to keep the Cold War going for another forty years, up until the Alien invasion of 2030."

"Some argued that the perpetual conflict saved humanity from going extinct, with the arms buildup and all," he interjected. Professor Victor nodded, "So you did study a bit? In the end, with so much potential and spirit we ended up as whores to aliens in order to win.

Speaking of wasted chances, I've never seen someone piss away so much potential so often. You had a promising career in the military. Then you screwed that up by running your mouth too much. Hell, you even got a second chance with a free ride through school, and you've managed to put that in certain jeopardy, too. Do you like being, as the ancients would say, a broken record? You seem to be playing the same sour notes over and over again."

"Telling someone to get over something and doing it are two different things," Alec moaned as he fought off the remnants of his hangover. Professor Victor gave him some water, and he slowly drank it. "Thanks."

The professor smiled, "No problem. Wouldn't want you to die from dehydration."

"I was hoping to go out with my boots on. Was I really that delusional?" Alec took another swig of the drink feeling more lightheaded than he was before. "Peace time is a bad time to join in," answered the professor.

"Here I was thinking peace was a good thing. I really didn't think the military would be that bureaucratic. I just wanted to be a tough guy for once instead of a victim," Alec kept drinking finishing the bottle, "This is counterproductive."

"The water or your line of thinking? You can have another bottle." Victor held out another bottle of water and Alec took a swig, "When will it kick in? I still feel woozy."

"The water, soon. As for your line of thinking, that's up to you. You already had two chances at life. What would you do with a third?" Victor asked as Alec finished the second bottle. "As you told me the ancients said, third time is the charm. If this is a fantasy life we're talking about, I would get even with the jerk wads that screwed me over and never get messed with again!"

Victor started laughing, "Well there's another saying from the ancient times: never say never." Alec laughed as he passed out in the chair.

"I need to cut down on my drinking," Alec groaned as he sat up in the dark room. He reached up to feel his head and touched a helmet. "What the?"

A light came on blinding him. He held his hands up to cover his eyes and felt plastic glasses covering them. They immediately started displaying text information to him. "Okay, this isn't the worst thing to happen to me after passing out," he said aloud, "But this is definitely not what I expected."

"Talking to yourself again?" Professor Victor asked him with glee in his voice. Alec stood up, "What in the hell is going on? Did you spike my drink?"

"No, you were just really hung over, so I took advantage of that opportunity to give you a test, pass or fail only," Victor told him as Alec franticly looked around. He caught his reflection in the glass of the door. In addition to the helmet and glasses he felt earlier, Alec had on an armored vest, boots, a parachute on his back, grenades, several magazines of ammo, a plasma knife, med kit, radio, plasma pistol and a plasma rifle with a grenade launcher attached. That's when he really panicked, "These are illegal as hell! How did you get a hold of all this shit?"

"A friend of mine," smiled the professor. "You're right about it being illegal. And about that test, the police are on their way. With the amount of priors you have, you wouldn't stand a chance in court. So you can either end up as someone's prison whore, or you can be the master for once. You've wanted this all your life. Now's your chance to be a tough guy for real. Do you have the balls to do it, or were you just talking out your ass earlier? Make up your mind." With that, Professor Victor exited the classroom.

Left alone in the room, Alec franticly looked around for any other exit besides the main door. He saw a thin set of windows up above, but he wouldn't be able to fit through. His heart started racing as he heard the footsteps of the police coming up to the door. As he scanned the room, his glasses changed vision allowing him to see through the wall. He saw the cops stacked up in the hallway, following one another toward the door. They had on similar equipment as he did, save the energy weapons.

Alec didn't see anything he could take cover behind

inside the room nor any viable place to hide. His mind raced thinking about what to do next. The idea of killing officers who were just doing their job didn't sit right with him, but going to prison didn't either. He took a closer look at the weapons they were holding, only lethal rounds. "Shit!" He gripped the pistol grip on the rifle, and he brought it up to his shoulder. As much dread as he had, he also felt excitement. Alec always wanted to be in a real fight. The police stopped just short of the door, and the lead officer went around to the other side. They were getting ready to breach. "Fuck it. I'm in the deep already. Might as well swim."

Alec pulled the rifle up to his cheek and a sight came up on his glasses showing him where he was aiming. He reached forward checking the grenade launcher attached to the rifle and flipped the selector switch to penetration mode. As one of the officers reached over to open the door, Alec fired a grenade round. The rifle jerked back into his shoulder as the round went into the door and sent a penetrating charge right through it. Soon the door came flying back at Alec. He stepped out of the way just in time, dodging it. The blast left a ring in his ears. Recovering quickly he ran out the door.

Alec slipped on the blood from the severed limbs on the floor, landing on his back. In shock he saw two of the officers were dead, and the others were wounded and crying in pain. A sickening smell of burnt meat clogged his nose as he tried getting up. He froze as more cops came around the corner with their weapons ready. Remaining as still as a stone, Alec waited for them to get close to him. One of the cops saw his rifle, but before he could aim, Alec had him lined up in his target display. With a spitting sound coming from the rifle, a puff of steam came from the officer's wound. He grunted as he dropped backwards.

Alec quickly moved his rifle, shooting the others in a full auto volley. Most of the shots hit their mark, but several missed. He held down the trigger so long that he ran out of ammo in the mag. He got up, pulling out his pistol and leaving his rifle to hang on a sling. Alec looked around the thin hallway for anyone else. Seeing no one, he quickly holstered his pistol and reloaded his rifle.

Alec went forward and changed the rate of fire from auto to semi. He kept his elbows close to his squared body and stayed on the balls of his feet. He saw an arrow pointing left inside his glasses. Without question, he followed it. After a quick peek around the corner, he moved as fast as he could down the hallway. He kept a steady pace and breathed as slowly as he could to try and lower his heart rate. It didn't help when he saw a radar display of all the officers closing in on him.

A warning flashed telling him to watch out for cameras. Alec looked up to see one looking down at him. He stared for a second and decided to smash it with his rifle butt. He knew it wouldn't really help, but it was the principle that mattered. He stopped just before coming up on an opening. In front of him were several civilians being rushed off and more cops coming in. The monitor told him to run for the picture window. It would be his escape. He pulled out all his hand held grenades and threw them out into the open. Ducking down, he waited for each one to go off, sending smoke and debris into the air.

With the sound of falling rubble and screaming, Alec threw two holo-projectors displaying images of himself running. After a couple of deep breaths, he charged out of the hall into the open bay. Bullets flew all around him as he sprinted away. Using the target display in his glasses, he shot from the hip. He pulled on the trigger over and over, hitting the officers right in the chest. He was almost to the window when a black and white police craft came into view. The hover jet looked like a bird of prey with the way its wings were angled forward. The fuselages were aerodynamic and had a quad machine gun mounted on the nose with two more machine gunners on the sides of the craft.

Alec leaped on top of a cop's shoulders, using him

to launch himself in the air. He fired off a grenade that broke the window apart and landed right into the cockpit of the aircraft. It went backward as the round went off sending the two side gunners out the door, plummeting to the forest below.

Alec went to the broken window, and the hover jet exploded above him, raining down fire and metal. He jumped. As he spread his arms out webbing appeared, almost like wings, allowing him to glide away from the blast. The sun came out from the clouds illuminating the glass towers against the green forest. It got bigger and bigger the further he went along. Alec deployed the parachute, trying to slow his descent. For some reason though, he wasn't slowing down. Alec saw the trees beneath him getting closer and closer and sighed, "This is going to hurt."

CHAPTER 2
TIME UNKNOWN
LOCATION IN GALAXY UNKNOWN
PANDORA
INFIRMARY

ALEC stumbled around as he reoriented himself. He rubbed his eyes as he yelled, "What the hell? Can I get a little warning next time?"

Yosemite kept on smiling as he played around with the empty vial, "What did you see?"

"I see an asshole!" Alec snapped at him. Yosemite took a step forward and asked again, "What did you see?"

Alec calmed himself the best he could and described what felt like a dream, "I was on a planet called Mars. Apparently I was a has-been who got dragged into something that was illegal by an old man who took advantage of me. Wait, I didn't phrase that right. That was a mistake."

"You were a mistake. For one, you were a 'never-was.' Being a has-been means that you were something at one time. You weren't. Just because you could run your mouth didn't make you anything. There is hope for you yet. Mistakes can be corrected with the right solution. Now you mentioned something about an old man. Nickolas Victor?"

"Didn't catch his first name, but yes, probably the same person. What about him?" Alec asked while leaning against the bulkhead. Doc offered him a drink. Remembering the water from Professor Victor, Alec refused, "No thanks. I'm good."

"You have no digestive system. This can't hurt you. It's just for comfort and a show for your mind, so drink up." Alec sighed and chugged the drink down. As he did he thought aloud, "You said I don't have a digestive system. What's left of me that's organic?"

"I was only able to save what was important. You should be thankful that we have similar priorities," Doc explained. Alec looked down and nodded his head, "Very good priorities indeed. Thanks. How come I know certain things like organs, priorities and fighting, yet I can't remember anything else?"

"Like I said, we saved what was important. Besides, the past should be let go. It can haunt us later on," Doc told him as he took away the empty cup and walked off. "Is everyone on this ship so cryptic?" Alec wondered.

"Lightens the mood. Seeing how you are up and lively, you'll be joining Squad Twelve for a mission. Get to know everyone again. Follow the arrow on your visual display, and you'll find them. They'll show you more of what is to be done now," said Yosemite as the alien finished his cigar and vanished into the shadows. Alec stood there bewildered, "He thinks I'm good to go on a mission. What the hell kind of standards do you all have for duty?"

Doc told him, "You just killed three people while unarmed and with no armor on. I think you'll do just fine on a mission." He pointed to a set of doors, "There's no gravity or air in the passageways right now. You'll need this."

He handed Alec a dark green suit that had a breathing apparatus, was air tight and had a mask that looked like a human skull. It was easy to slip on, fitting over his boots and coveralls. The suit was surprisingly snug. Once he was dressed, he thought of something, "If I don't need to breathe, then why do I need an airtight suit?"

"You can still get turned inside out in a vacuum. It's one of the things I'm still working on. Also, close the first door before you open the second one. Wouldn't want to get decompressed in here."

"Place feels overly compressed to me. Guess I'll see

you later." Alec went for the door, opened it up and went inside the air lock as quickly as possible. He saw the airlock was painted white and there were "Z's" on the doors. It felt oddly familiar to him. Alec closed the door behind him and went forward as the air started venting out with a hissing sound that echoed in the small space. He looked up to see a red light that turned green once the door was safe to open. Alec pulled it and went drifting into the air. He had to pull himself out into a passageway that looked like a set of tunnels.

The door closed and Alec followed the arrow in his display. There were grooves like a ladder allowing him to move easily. There were also parts of the passageway that were flat. "Must be for when gravity is activated," he thought. There were sets of numbers at various intervals to help people find their way through the ship. Alec had to go through three more airlocks before he made it to where the arrow was guiding him. A sign above the opening said "Classroom." Alec went through the airlock and saw four people sitting down with one other person upfront and leaning against a podium. All of them looked tired and worn out. They had armored plates lying around them, and their suits looked like they were a couple tears away from falling apart completely. Some of them had wounds that hadn't fully healed yet. One of them asked, "Who the hell is this jackass?"

Once the doors behind him closed, he pulled his mask off hoping one of them would tell him who he was. Instead they only asked questions. A woman stood up and said, "You? How did you survive?"

"I got better... apparently," Alec told her feeling a bit of hostility from the group, especially the man that stared at Alec like he wanted him dead. Another woman sitting down said, "I knew Doc was talented, but I didn't think you'd recover from having half your head blown off."

Alec's eyes went wide when he heard this, "Really? That does sound hard to survive. I guess that explains my amnesia and looks. I should let you all know, I don't know who the hell any of you are. I'm Alec, and I was sent down here to get to know you all again."

"Are you fucking kidding me?" the woman with thin eyes leaning against the podium grumbled. Out of all the people in the room, she was the only one who Alec felt any familiarity with. She had black hair that hung down to her shoulders, an almost perfect hourglass body and tanned skin. She introduced herself with a terse smile, "I'm Kathryn. Everyone else?" She motioned for the others to do the same. "Jane," said the woman closest to him. She looked similar to Kathryn but with red hair, light skin, wide eyes, and freckles. "Mira Price," the woman with blonde hair and blue eyes said. "Cullen McCormick," the man with slicked back red hair, thin eyes and burnt red skin said. He looked similar to Duncan, the man from his flashback. "Yeager 'Bomb' Marley, motherfucker!" said the man who had been staring at him since he entered the room. Alec noticed the visible hate in his eyes and also that they looked a bit alike. Cullen asked "Okay. Now that we got this circle jerk over with, what now?"

Alec wondered out loud, "That is a good question. What happens now?"

Mira sighed, "Alec, I guess, do you really not remember anything?"

"Wait a second. Why are they putting a man who can't remember anything into a combat team? He's a hazard and could get us killed." Jane asked, pointing out the obvious.

Kathryn tapped on a holo-pad and a wall monitor lit up showing everyone the fight Alec was in earlier. He felt chills as he saw himself ruthlessly dispatch each of his attackers. Kathryn explained, "As you all can see, he can still fight. This room used to have more people in it. It's not every day that we get a replacement. As much as I hate doing this, we've got to do some regrouping. Besides, we have to move on from our failures eventually," Kathryn sighed as she pulled up holo-projections of ships and personnel. "Okay, Alec. Besides fighting, what else do you remember?"

"Just that I first got involved after a night of drinking too much and getting extorted by Victor." Before he could get another word out, Yeager leaped out of his seat. He would've reached Alec if it wasn't for Mira and Jane restraining him. "Don't you dare talk about him!"

"Yeager, not now!" reminded Kathryn, "Alec, I'll give you an abridged version of everything that happened from the year 2189 to 2214."

"That was twenty five years ago?" Alec asked bewildered by how much time had passed. Mira sighed, "Yes. That day was the beginning of the uprising. We call ourselves Spartans because…why the hell not?"

Jane rubbed her head, "It's because we wanted to have an intimidating name."

Kathryn slammed the podium, "Stay on subject! We don't have all day! For starters, we've been on the run ever since we lost our last major battle. We're hiding out in the asteroid belt of the Sol system. We don't know how many or if any other ships made it out of that blood bath. We're waiting to see what our Stallion friend has in mind for us next."

"The alien I met in the infirmary?" Alec asked. Cullen told him, "That's racist! But yes, Yosemite is our only hope at this point. Why he didn't help us in the battle, I don't know."

"That's as much up to speed as we can bring you, Alec. Now did Yosemite say anything insightful?" Kathryn asked. He thought about it, "Just violence isn't the question; it's the solution."

"Really?" Kathryn asked. "Yes," Yosemite said standing in front of the airlock. Cullen let out a screaming gasp as he fell out of his seat. Yeager sighed, "Do you always have to do that?"

Kathryn snapped, "You can pop up whenever you want, but not when we need you? Where were you when we were getting our asses kicked?"

"We didn't feel that intervention was needed. You had everything going for you from technology to numbers. Tell me, how did things go wrong?" Yosemite asked looking at her already knowing the answer. "I don't know," Kathryn answered, "Everything seemed to be going so well. If I had to pinpoint the exact moment when things went wrong, it was right after Squad Thirteen failed its objective. The whole squad was wiped out…except one." She looked over at Alec. He pointed to himself, "I fucked up?"

Yosemite's shark like teeth formed an intimidating frown, "Yes, you did, not me, not the Stallions. After all the resources, training, and support we gave you, what did we get? Only failure. So much for the motto of 'Unfucking defeated.' I liked that motto. Thanks to you Spartan posers, we now have a blotch on our track record. Yet, there is a chance for redemption."

Kathryn looked up at him sighing, "I'm listening."

"The reason he is here..." He pointed at Alec, "...is because he saw some important information just before he lost all his memory. If we can find out how the enemy used the slip gate against us, we could do the same against them and take back this system that should be ours. Need I remind you of what the Vegan puppets did?" Yosemite asked looking around the room. Alec had to ask, "Vegans? You mean those nature loving vegetarians?"

Everyone in the room started laughing. Mira asked smiling, "How is it you remember that but not your own name?"

Yosemite went on smiling again, "These animals are more annoying and deceptive than the vegans you're thinking of." He tapped on the holo-pad and a tall, amphibious looking being appeared on the screen. It didn't have a mouth and had gills on each side of its neck. The color of its skin shifted from green to gray. Yosemite continued, "These are the assholes that sponsored the puppet government known as the 'Alliance.' We also have

32

the opportunity to turn the tables on said puppet government. We'll take Alec down memory lane while sabotaging the Alliance. This will buy time for Spartan Corps to regroup and rebuild. Sound reasonable?"

"Can't really argue with that. Where to first?" Kathryn asked waiting for instructions. Yosemite smiled tapping on the holo-pad. An image of Mars in all its blue and green glory appeared, "We are going to get an old friend back. We'll find him on this planet."

"How are we going to sneak over there with at least half of Alliance's space navy hunting us down?" Jane asked. Yosemite went on, "There's an Alliance Raven drop ship that crashed in our hanger bay. We'll be using it to reach Mars."

Cullen stood up, "You're joining us?"

"What fun would it be on the side lines?" Alec replied. "Good," Cullen looked over at me, "I'll help you down memory lane."

Yeager retorted, "I think giving him memory loss would be more fun." Yosemite almost laughed. He had to cover his mouth to keep from smiling, "We've been thought a lot today. Know that no matter what, we can bounce back. I'll give you all some time to recuperate. Use it wisely. Be ready by this time tomorrow. See you then." He went out the airlock. Everyone else got up dragging their gear as they took turns going out of the airlock. Eventually it was just Alec and Mira alone inside the room. She held her hand on the door, "What's it like?"

"Memory loss? Feels like I lived life on fast forward and missed everything in the black fuzzy haze. I really hate being lost and confused. Also, it doesn't help to know that I screwed everyone over. At least I got a second chance, right?" he asked thinking about his whole situation. Mira walked forward towards Alec. She then leaned up and kissed him on the lips. He didn't mind. One of her hands went behind Alec's head massaging his neck. He dropped his face mask as he instinctually gave her a hug. In between kisses, he muttered, "Guess I didn't forget everything."

"Let me help you remember." Mira stripped down, and Alec followed suit. She slipped her tongue into his mouth as they went down to the floor. Mira straddled him, and he felt a warm sensation as he entered her. Despite the implants and augmentation, he was still feeling pleasure, and so was she. Alec used his legs to thrust upwards as she used her hips to thrust down. Alec propped himself up with one arm and massaged her body with the others. She gasped after every thrust, and he breathed heavily. He looked at Mira and for a brief second saw Kathryn on top of him instead. Weird as it was, it didn't faze him too much. Alec flipped Mira over and thrust down into her.

She smiled as they both started nearing their climax. Mira's body went into a spasm as Alec felt his grand release and rolled off of her. Before he could finish enjoying the moment, she stuck a syringe filled with green liquid into his eye. "Not again!" Alec thought as images swirled around him.

Chapter 3
Rising
2189
Mars
Limburger Forest

"Wake up!" screamed Duncan as he slapped Alec over and over again. He was about to hit him again, when Alec reached up and grabbed his arm, "I'm awake!"

"About time! You've been out for two days!" Duncan pulled him up on his feet. Alec saw Duncan wore the same combat gear he did, "Victor screw you over, too?"

Duncan looked down and shook his head, "No. I volunteered."

"Really?" Alec asked looking surprised. Duncan nodded his head, "Hell yeah. I'm sick of all Earth's corruption and want to make a change, even if shit gets blown up."

"Okay, nice to see you on the team. I'll forget the whole, you kicking me out of the apartment thing." Alec pulled his rifle up and checked his gear. It was dusk, and the sun was going down. The trees moved gently as the wind whistled through them. The sky was getting dimmer by the minute. Duncan laughed, "Second chances for us all."

"Is your family safe?" Alec asked slightly concerned. "Wife goes by her maiden name. Son is still loyal. He'll be fine. Follow me, I'll bring you up to speed," Duncan answered.

The two of them walked through the forest passing by trees neatly set in rows of threes reminiscent of the ones on Earth. Duncan marveled, "Can you believe at one time this was an inhospitable desert?"

"I guess. Terraforming is fascinating as shit. What are you looking at?" Alec wondered as he saw him focused on his holo-pad. Duncan laughed, "You. Look at this."

He pulled up a screen showing Alec's jump out of the tower. "You're famous! There was a massive man hunt for you. Locked down the whole tower just to get your ass. Congratulations, Alec. We're criminals now!"

"You seem to be enjoying this a little too much," Alec looked at him with worry in his eyes. Duncan laughed, "That's a lot coming from a hell raiser like you! Don't lie; a part of you thinks it's fun to have the whole system against you. You've talked about it your whole life, and now you get to live it! Life is good!"

The scenery seemed to add weight to what he was saying. They came out onto a cliff, and watched as stairs appeared in the sky. Alec smiled, "Us against the system. When do we attack?"

Duncan slapped him on the back. Alec felt the parachute was still on. "Now."

He gave Alec a push off the cliff and jumped off himself. They both deployed the webbing between their limbs, guiding their descent. Alec gasped as the night grew darker. He felt joy leaping into the unknown. Alec followed Duncan as they headed to a set of lights in the horizon. They got near an opening and deployed their parachutes. Both landed softly on the grass field and pulled the chutes back into their packs. Alec laughed as he walked forward in a daze, "I think I can get into this."

"Good. You're going to love what's next," Duncan pulled him along as they jogged toward a massive factory. This was unlike any factory Alec remembered. A mirrored dome sat in the middle of the forest with magnetic trail lines coming out at six points. The dome was surrounded by a fence, and security guards patrolled the perimeter. Alec went along with it laughing, "Breaking and entering? Never thought you'd pull that stick out of your ass. Where you'd learn to do something like this?"

"Never thought you'd get a stick up yours. Things

change," he asserted. Both of them laughed quietly. Duncan requested, "When the guards pass by, give me a boost over the fence. Got it? Let's see what's on the other side."

Alec and Duncan slowly moved to the fence as the guard passed by not noticing them. Alec got there first, steadied himself and put his hands out. Duncan ran up and jumped onto Alec's hands as he pushed up. Duncan landed on top and held on. He reached down with one hand, and Alec leaped up grabbing Duncan. Alec grabbed the fence and pulled himself to the other side. He landed without making a sound, and Duncan came down right next to him.

Alec's heart raced as they quickly snuck behind the oblivious guard. The adrenaline felt good going through his body as they tipped toward the door. The glasses on their faces automatically tapped into the factory's security system allowing them to see exactly what the cameras saw. Alec and Duncan moved accordingly to avoid being seen. Their weapons were pointed low to the ground and ready. Each leaned against the wall on opposite sides of the doorway. Duncan placed a hacking device onto the lock giving them access. Alec quickly ran in and swept the area for targets as Duncan followed, "Clear."

"All clear. Put your weapon on silent mode!"

Duncan whispered loudly. Alec quickly made the adjustments as they kept going. The hallways were colored a plain gray and had white lighting. Windows on either side showed an assembly line of androids being constructed. It was reminiscent of the old car assemblies. Most of the androids were female. Alec looked closer and realized they all looked just like Kathryn. He remarked, "I think I lost my virginity to an android from here."

"Not to mention a good many nights, too. Come on," Duncan motioned for him to follow as they kept going down the hall. They ducked behind a corner to avoid another guard and snuck past him. "Where are we going?" Alec whispered.

"Main computer core. Just keep up." Duncan went against the wall with Alec following. He put another hacking device onto the door, and it popped. They swept the next room. It was clear, too. They went to the main holo-console, and Duncan started tampering with it, "That was easy. I am little disappointed. Security here sucks."

Alec laughed, "What did you expect? There hasn't been a major conflict or even a major break-in for decades. People are going to be lax. Weren't we?"

Duncan paused, "Not going to lie, I slept a couple times on watch."

Alec looked around, "Look a fridge!"

"Now's not the time for eating," Duncan told him as he started tapping on the holo-controls. Alec pulled out two golden beers with the alcohol potency of a bottle of hard liquor, "What about drinking?"

"Fuck it," Duncan grabbed one. He took a swig and kept hitting the glowing buttons. The screen showed him the changes being made. Alec opened his drink and asked, "What are you doing?"

"Reprogramming the clones and AIs to be on our side. This will spread through the system like a virus making our cause a real force to deal with," Duncan explained as he finished loading up said virus. "That was easy."

"That's what she said," Alec snickered. Both of them started laughing. "Grab more of the beer. We'll need something to drink when we go into space."

"Isn't that a bad idea? What about the sickness?" Alec started pulling out the drinks. Duncan finished his drink and grabbed another one, "Going to get sick no matter what. May as well enjoy it."

The two of them brazenly walked out of the room drinking the extra strong beer, not caring if they got caught. As they walked toward the stairway, they went right past a guard. Alec raised his bottle smiling. Alec and

Duncan walked past the surprised guard, stumbling as the alcohol kicked in. Suddenly they heard the chirp of the guard's radio. Alec turned around and threw his empty bottle at the guard's head. He was knocked out instantly, falling on his back. "How are we going to explain this one?" Duncan asked. Alec walked over cracking open another drink, "Looks like someone can't handle their alcohol. Drinking on the job, what a shit bag!"

Duncan laughed almost spilling his beer. Alec got back up tossing him another drink, "Here's to revolution!"

"Fucking revolution!" Both of them cheered as they started walking up the stairs. It took them an hour to get to the top. By the time they did Alec started throwing up. Duncan gasped while holding his chest, "In retrospect, drinking wasn't such a good idea!"

"Don't be a bitch! It was worth it." Alec leaned back over throwing up. The two of them stumbled toward a transport sitting up on the roof. Duncan came to a realization, "You idiot! They'll be able to get your DNA off that!"

Alec lifted a finger up. "Wait. I have an idea," he whispered as he pointed to a security guard making his rounds. Alec opened a bottle of beer and snuck up behind him. In one shift motion, he forced the bottle down the guard's throat from behind and dragged him back to the puke pile. The guard started gagging as Alec laughed, "Someone has a weak stomach!"

The guard began vomiting uncontrollably. "Problem solved. They'll have a hard time figuring out who I am with cross contamination. We weren't seen on the security cameras, right?" Alec asked. Duncan tapped away on his holo-pad, "No. I don't think anyone is going to believe this drunk anyway."

Both of them started laughing as they walked towards the launch platform. There a shuttle waited for them. It was a simple delta wing shaped shuttle similar to the spacecraft of old. After opening the hatch they leaped inside and made their way into the cockpit. Alec took the pilot's seat and Duncan sat in the co-pilot's chair. "Do you know how to fly?" Duncan asked.

Alec paused for a moment, "Shit. Didn't think about that, now did we?"

"Are you kidding me? We just went through all this crap, and we can't even fly this thing?" Duncan snapped in frustration and panic. Alec leaned back against the seat thinking. He looked at the cargo manifest and saw something that caught his eye, "Maybe we can get someone who can."

"What do you mean?" Duncan asked as Alec hopped out of the seat. He motion for Duncan to follow, and they walked back into the transport. Lights came on illuminating their path as they got to the hibernation pods. Each one housed an AI or clone waiting to be programmed. "We can get one of them to fly this thing," Alec announced, "Wouldn't hurt to have some pretty faces on the flight either." Duncan started tapping away on the holo-controls, reprogramming one of the pods. Alec leaned back reading the preselected names, "Kathryn, Lauren, Jane 68, and Jane 60," Alec started cracking up, "She is going to be hating life."

Duncan looked over and cracked up himself, "Sucks having a number as a last name."

"Ever feel wrong about using clones and AIs for our own amusement?" Alec suddenly thought. Duncan shrugged as he went on to the next one, "Well, I do fear the day one of them becomes sentient and leads an apocalypse. At least now, they'll be uprising with us instead of against us."

"Kill the rich and corrupt. Free the exploited. I'm starting to like this revolution more and more. So, are these ladies going to know enough right off the bat to fly this thing?" Alec asked as Duncan made some last minute adjustments, "Mostly. Their minds have to process information that would normally take years to learn. Lucky for us it will only take them seconds. The AIs will pilot.

The clones were a little more complex, so I made them into fighters. Shame that every operation isn't going to be this easy."

"Where would the fun in that be? I'm getting bored already. Can we wake them yet?" Alec started getting anxious. Duncan smiled, "Good to go."

The pods opened up, and the women walked out. The two clones held their heads processing the information being given to them. The two AIs walked up to Alec. Both of them looked almost identical, and both had on skin tight jumpsuits. Lauren asked, "Got a ship for us to fly?"

"Yeah. Cockpit is just down that way," Alec pointed. "Thanks."

They walked off taking control of the transport. It hummed to life. Suddenly they felt heavier as the ship lifted off into the air. Alec walked up to one of the clones, "Are you okay?"

She looked dazed and confused as she struggled to stand up straight. Alec noticed a holo-image of the outside of the ship. "Come, let me show you the world."

He motioned for her to come over. She slowly walked to him and they both looked out as the stars became brighter as they got higher into the atmosphere. She gasped at the sight, taking in everything at once. Alec told her, "Welcome to life. Make yours worth living."

The other clone asked, "Where are we going?"

Duncan pointed out, "To the Pandora. She'll be visible right about..." A ship suddenly came out from the darkness. The Pandora was massive compared to the transport. She looked to be about five kilometers long, two kilometers wide, and a kilometer and a half tall. Her body was shaped like a cross between a whale and a four pointed star. The ship was painted black with almost no windows and no exterior lights. The engines were located on the outer triangular edges of the ship, and the weapons were spread throughout the exterior. Missile ports, torpedo launchers and plasma cannons were tucked inside the vessel. She could fire in any direction at any time and move in any direction. They headed for the center of the ship as the black hull encompassed everyone's view. "Those AIs know what they are doing right?" Alec asked worried as he didn't see any openings as they got closer and closer to the ship. "I did my best," he replied

They both gasped as it looked like they were going to crash. Suddenly a hanger bay appeared, and the AI guided them in for a safe landing. The transport turned around, and they saw a holographic image of the ship's hull being replaced with a closing door. One of the clones smiled, "Nice. I think I'm going to like it here."

The door opened up, and Victor walked in smiling, "You made it. About time."

He look younger than before and was wearing an armored suit. The two AIs walked back into the compartment. One of them gave Alec the middle finger, "Thought I would crash; didn't you?"

Victor laughed, "You know how to treat a lady; don't you?"

"How was I supposed to know part of the hull was a hologram? And how the hell did you get a fucking dreadnought on a professor's salary, not to mention all the equipment that's on here? Never thought you had it in you," Alec laughed.

"I didn't think you could pull yourself together to get here," Victor responded. "Yet here we are. Everyone deserves another chance to get things right. Come, let me introduce you to a friend of mine."

The seven of them walked outside into the hanger where several fighters and transports were being worked on by crew members wearing green coveralls. "Greetings," a voice boomed next to them. They looked over and saw Yosemite smiling, "We have much to do, yet time is something we can take for once." His smile went away as he started sniffing the air. "Are you two drunk?"

Both Duncan and Alec stood there guilty as they

cracked a smile, "Well, as you said, time was on our side."

Yosemite turned to Victor, "These were the ones you picked to join us?"

"What better people to choose than ones with nothing to lose?" Victor pointed out. Yosemite sighed, "We have time. Get them ready."

He walked off as Victor turned his attention back to Alec and Duncan. "If you two were able to sneak in and out of a low security factory, maybe you two could do the same on a larger scale sober. I'll show you two to a birthing pod to rest. You're both going to need it."

Alec and Duncan looked at each other nodding as they stepped out of the transport. Victor started saying, "Watch your…" It was too late. Alec slipped, falling right on his face. Victor sighed, "Step."

Chapter 4
Jailbreak
2214
Orbit of Mars
Transport

ALEC woke up on a transport. He was laying on the ground in a fully armored suit. It felt like he was wearing weighted clothing. Alec lifted up a skeleton mask to look inside the container area with his own eyes. Cullen, Kathryn, Jane 69, Mira, and Yeager were sitting around, also in new armored suits. All of them might have had the same pistol side arm, but they all had their own primary weapon. Cullen had a SMG submachine gun, Kathryn and Jane had assault rifles, Mira had a sniper rifle and Yeager had a shotgun cannon. All the weapons used plasma rounds and could be adjusted depending on how much power each shot needed. The weapons looked like they could be used as blunt instruments as well. Alec slowly sat up feeling sore all over. He looked over at Mira, "If you wanted it rough, why didn't you say so?"

"Just wanted to help you remember, even if it hurt you," she smiled. He couldn't help but feel a little creeped out by this. Yeager laughed, "Can I hurt him? For his memory?"

Alec got tired of his crap and stood up saying, "Going to bark all day little doggy, or are you going to bite?"

Yeager smiled as he got up. Kathryn quickly got in between them, "Both of you calm down! We'll be committing violence soon enough. Yeager, no more antagonizing him. Got it?"

"Fine." He sat back down and went back to checking his weapons. Kathryn walked over, "Sorry about that. He's a hot head."

"As long as he doesn't do it again. So you're an AI?" Alec asked remembering the last flash of memories. She nodded, "Yeah. Guess you saw when I was first activated all those years ago."

"You look and act so human," he said admiring the way she was. He couldn't help but feel fond of her. She seemed to be the only pleasant thing that felt familiar. "Thanks. I was made that way. If it wasn't for you and Duncan..." She paused as Cullen looked over, "... I would have just been another object. Glad I was able to become something more than that."

"Guess I feel the same. I was a never-was apparently," Alec laughed thinking about it. It felt good to reminisce. "Those were the days. We spent a lot of time training and hibernating, all for the uprising. That had a quick crash."

"Don't worry. We can try again right?" Alec asked trying to cheer her up. It worked. She smiled, "Live to fight another day."

He smiled, too, "So speaking of fighting, what are we doing?"

She explained, "We're going to a prison that we think has Victor and some other comrades of ours." Alec asked, "Guess this isn't a regular visit?"

Yosemite walk down from the cockpit. His armored suit almost made Alec jump. His head was covered in a plain, round gray sphere helmet that sat on top of his black armored suit. "You would guess correctly. Did you go over the plan yet?"

Kathryn pulled up a hologram of the prison and the surrounding area. The prison was a simple box with four towers on each corner and a fence going between them. Yosemite explained, "This transport's IFF will allow us to slip in undetected. I'll create a distraction from the north allowing you all to insert yourselves into the compound. Mira will go up on the southwest towers providing sniper support. Jane, you'll assist. Kathryn, you'll lead Cullen, Yeager, and Alec into the prison itself from the lower security end and work your way up.

Free all the prisoners, but only take the one we came for. Once he's secured, head to the roof. The transport will first pick up the sniper team, then extract you from the roof. After that I'll meet up with you outside the perimeter for extraction. If Victor is too beat up to be extracted, we'll put him out of his misery. Let's hope he hasn't cracked yet. Any questions?"

No one said anything. The back door opened with the air going out as Yosemite grabbed a rocket launcher and what looked like a Gatling gun. "Good luck."

He leaped out of the transport into the dark of night without hesitation. Soon flashes of light could be seen from below. "Jane, Mira. You're up."

The two of them went to the door and waited for the tower to come into view. Once it did the two of them leaped out, killed the guards and took up positions. "We're up!"

The four of them lined up, weapons ready. Yeager and Alec covering the left and Kathryn and Cullen covering the right. The ground seemed to rise up to them as they landed. "Go!"

They bolted out of the transport into the open.

Alec felt light as a feather while running with the armored suit. Yeager took the lead and fired away at the building, blowing a door off its hinges. Meanwhile, Mira and Jane were picking off the guards. They dropped dead in pairs. They kept the path for them clear. Yeager went in going left. Alec followed clearing the right. Sweeping his weapons from the corner, he pulled the trigger when his weapon lined up with a guard. They let out a quick grunt before dropping to the floor. The SMG Alec was using was relatively quiet. The gun shots were drowned out by the alarms. Alec heard Yeager yelling, "Clear!"

"All clear!" he replied as Kathryn and Cullen cleared the next room. Several shots were fired off followed quickly by the thuds of dead bodies hitting the floor. "Clear!"

"All clear!" Once they heard that they went in. Alec looked down seeing the guards only had on coveralls with basic body armor on: a vest, knee pads, elbow pads, and a helmet. They stepped over the dead while moving on. Cullen peeked into the next room with a camera, "There's a dozen guards in the next room. Once we clear that out, we can gain access to the security room."

Kathryn broke out some holo-decoys and threw them into the room. The guards shot at the images of light as the team charged in. Yeager's blasts ripped apart the energy shields the guards carried in a bright flash of light. Before they recovered, they got hit again. As Yeager and Kathryn finished the initial guards, more came charging in from the opposite side of the room. Cullen and Alec picked them off as they came through the, door taking turns firing. After killing several of them they caught on and stopped coming though.

Kathryn threw a grenade into the next room and heard brief screams before the explosion silenced them. The four of them went to the security room entrance and lined up against the wall. Kathryn opened the door, and Alec went in first. There was only one guard inside. He fired away with his pistol with Alec's shields taking the hits. Alec hit him three times in the torso, and he went down. "Clear!"

"All clear. Cullen, hack the computer while Alec, Yeager and I cover the doorway," Kathryn ordered. Cullen placed his hacking device over the holo-emitter and started accessing all the prison's systems. "I've turned the air defense turrets against the hostiles, and I've opened every cell in the prison," he said. Alec looked back seeing the security footage of prisoners in red suits charging out into the hallways killing the guards that imprisoned them. "Where's Victor?" Alec asked.

"He's in the maximum security section of the

prison. I can't hack any of those systems. Someone is going to have to go to the other side and blast him out," replied Cullen.

Kathryn ordered, "Yeager, Alec got get him. Cullen and I will stay behind. We'll open the doors and disable the auto turrets. Better yet, turn them against the guards. Don't shoot each other."

They both looked at each other. Alec asked, "We're not going to have any issues are we?"

"Don't get into my line of fire, and you won't get shot," he told him. Alec stood aside, "After you."

Yeager went first, and Alec followed right behind him. They went into the cell block of rioting prisoners. The guards weren't getting shown any mercy. Each one was getting kicked over and over again by the prisoners. Yeager fired his shotgun cannon in the air, getting their attention, "Who wants to blow this place the hell up?"

They cheered. Yeager started handing them grenades. Alec even gave out a couple out, too. He pointed, "The armory is that way. Have fun!"

They cheered as they went off on their rampage. Thanks to the riot, the path was cleared out. All that was in front of them were several dead guards and burning blankets. They kept going down the corridor, running into no resistance. As they both ran towards the high security area, Alec asked, "What did I do to piss you off?"

"You did things. Things that really pissed me off. Let's leave it at that," Yeager told him with anger rattling in his voice. Alec sighed, "Not like that's vague or anything. Fuck it. Let's just get this guy and get out."

"That guy you mention so lightly was the closest thing I had to a father. Watch your damned mouth!" They came upon an open door and took positions on both sides. The sound of the auto turrets boomed as they waited for them to turn off. Alec looked over at Yeager feeling dismay. He thought about saying something else, but he didn't seem to be reasonable. Before they went into the next room they heard Cullen warning, "The turrets are on indiscriminate fire."

"Good!" Yeager went in. Alec followed watching him blast apart the turrets. They exploded into a flash of sparks after being hit with smoke rising from the wreckage. They both went on to the next room making it to the last door. It was welded shut from the inside. "Cullen, do you have eyes?"

"There are twenty guards in there all aiming at the door. That's the only way in. Say the word, and I can cut the power," he told us. Alec placed a thermal charge on the door. He motion with his fingers a countdown to three. Once three was counted off, he set off the explosive opening the door. "Now!"

The lights went out as the two of them charged into the room. They used the holo-decoys to draw fire. Their vision shifted to night allowing them to see. Yeager charged forward blasting away as Alec picked off the ones he'd missed. They went from body to body shooting it in the head making sure the guard was dead. "Clear!"

"All clear!" Yeager went to the cell door and blasted the lock off. He slammed the door open with a violent bang and yelled, "Victor!"

He pulled him out. Victor looked old, skinny, and beaten up. Alec went over to him, "Don't worry. We'll have you back on Pandora in time for chow."

He looked up at Alec and gasped, "You!"

Yeager grabbed his hand, "I'll explain later. Let's go!"

The three of them went back the way they came. Alec radioed to the team, "We got the package, heading to extraction!"

Yosemite's voice suddenly came over, "Enemy reinforcements coming in. Heading to main extraction!"

"Great," Alec led the way as Yeager carried Victor along. Cullen, Mira, Jane and Kathryn ran towards them as they were being chased by enemy soldiers. Alec took cover and fired back doing his best to cover them. The four rushed up the stairway. Kathryn grabbed Alec, "They got Mechs closing in. We need to be out of here!"

Alec followed, going up the stairs as fast as he could with plasma shots cracking around him. Jane dropped a grenade, blowing up a second set of the stairs behind them. The metal screeched and the stairwell collapsed in the flames. It bought them enough time to get to the roof. The night seemed well lit with all the fires burning. Down below the prisoners were being slaughtered by the oncoming troops. The ground rocked as the giant machines came closer. The turrets that Cullen hacked were being destroyed one by one. Yosemite came leaping onto the roof firing away with his Gatling gun as part of another roof collapsed nearby. He walked backward towards the team, motioning everyone to move. From above, the transport came flying in. It wasn't stopping. Once it got close enough, Yosemite yelled, "Jump!"

One by one, the team leaped up into the transport. Alec was second to last to leap. It started ascending before he could get to it. He grabbed the door, holding on for dear life. Jane was right below him. He reached down, grabbing her hand as they went up into the air. Alec felt his muscles being stretched as he gripped Jane with all the strength he had.

He saw the Mechs closing in. They looked like

giant armored humans strapped with weapons. Their hands carried the heaviest weapons. The Mechs fired in the air missing the transport and aiming for holo-decoys. There were several flak rounds that went off around them as the transport went higher in the air. Finally, someone grabbed Alec's arm pulling he and Jane both up. Once they both in, the door closed and everyone breathed a sigh of relief. Victor was having a conversation with Yosemite. He suddenly started laughing. Alec leaned against one of the chairs and took off his mask. Jane came over, "Thanks."

"Any time," he told her. Alec thought he would have a high heart rate, but most of his organs were now artificial. They all sat there as the transport kept rocking. "Do we always have close calls like that?" he asked.

Jane smiled getting close to Alec, "Only when the call is worth answering."

He cracked a smile, too. Yeager threw his weapon down in between them, "I saved your ass multiple times. Are you going to answer my call?"

Jane grumbled. Alec stood up pushing him back, "Fucking asshole! Tell me not to mess with you, but you keep it up with me? What? Did I fuck your mother or something?"

The last thing Alec remembered seeing was a fist flying into his face.

AWAKENING

CHAPTER 5
PRACTICE
2209
JUPITER'S ASTEROID BELT
SPARTA SPACE STATION
SIMULATOR ARENA

ALEC huffed and puffed as he tried to drink some water. Everyone was fully geared up in their armored suits training in a simulator. Lauren yelled, "Got to do that faster next time!"

"We've been working on this for years, literally, and we've gotten our time of taking over the Alliance freight down to twenty two minutes with acceptable losses. How's that not impressive?" Duncan moaned as he started vomiting. Jane 68 hit him over the head, "I'm not an acceptable loss!"

"No one is expendable at this phase! Duncan, you need to stop rushing your hacks. You keep running into firewalls. Fred, you need to grow a pair and stop cowering! Nick, you need to stop being so oblivious to your situation.

Mindy, stop sweeping your comrades with your weapon! Jane, don't get shot by Mindy. Bryan, stop rushing into every room! Tara, take it easy on the explosives. Alisa, stop wasting ammo, and Alec, stop being so finicky with ammo!" Lauren ordered.

Alec asked in an annoyed sigh, "Call me out on my impatience, but when are we doing this for real?"

"I'm not supposed to tell you this, but next week," Lauren revealed while looking over her shoulder. Everyone paused for a second when they heard this. She continued, "This is what we've been working for. We only have to get this right once. When we do, the Alliance is fucked. It's been a long day, and for what it's worth, you guys did well. Take the rest of the day off. We get our final orders tomorrow. Dismissed."

Everyone started limping towards the shower as they took off their armored gear. They all stunk of sweat after training all day. Inside the locker room everyone stripped down without paying much attention to each other's exposed bodies. They bagged up their dirty clothing and cleaned up their armored suits before hopping into the shower. Each of them breathed a sigh of relief as the piping hot water cleaned them off. Alec asked, "Has it really been twenty years?"

"Not really. Time passes by slower here than it does

on Earth. Isn't that weird?" Fred pointed out. Nick snapped, "That explains why it feels like we've been here twenty fucking years!"

"I thought it was because we've been doing the same drills over and over again. I swear, sometimes I feel like I'm in a time loop," Duncan muttered. Bryan cried, "Not again!"

Tara laughed, "You do know what the ancients said about dropping the soap, right?"

Mindy told her, "His water turned cold on him again. Never believed in jinxes until I met him. It doesn't help that we're Squad Thirteen either."

"Lauren, why do you even sweat? You're an AI." Jane asked. She answered, "I was programmed to sweat. Besides, I like showering."

Everyone started filing out of the shower to dry off leaving only Alisa and Alec. "So now we know why AIs like to keep their hygiene up like the rest of us. Learning so much!" she remarked.

Alisa shut off the water and grabbed a towel, "You're wondering why I'm here still?" "Yeah, I am." Alec followed her to her locker. She confessed, "I'm not here for you. You're just a hook up buddy. I'm here because Victor asked, and I followed."

"Did you two hook up, too?" Alec asked with a

touch of envy in his voice. Alisa quickly put on her green coveralls and closed up her locker. "Yes. What of it? We were never in a real relationship. We just hung out. Besides, you're a flake when it comes to lovers."

Alec was caught off guard. He gave up, "Got me there."

She smiled and tapped him on the chest, "Come on. Get dressed. They're giving us organic meat for dinner. Guess the mission really is on."

Alec felt his stomach rumble and quickly got dressed. The squad met up at their usual table in the mess hall. Everyone sat down together and started eating. Duncan smiled, "Haven't had food this good since Mars."

Jane added, "I haven't had food this good... ever."

"Got to ask, why do you eat again? Programmed?" Fred asked Lauren. "Sort of, it's to make me act more human, and I like the sensation of eating," she answered.

Mindy asked, "On behalf of humanity, sorry for all the stupid questions."

"Better stupid questions than ending up working at some strip joint. I count myself as lucky," Lauren told her taking a drink. Bryan spat out his food, "How the hell is there a hair in my food?"

Nick sighed, "You're going to get us all killed with your bad luck."

"Don't worry. His bad luck generally only hurts him. So as long as he suffers more in this victory, we'll be safe!" Tara smirked at him. Alisa shook her head, "Whatever happened to leave no one behind?"

"You've left me behind on several occasions." Alec pointed out. Alisa smiled, "You said you liked my behind."

Lauren slammed the table, "Please, nothing dirty at the table. We already have to deal with Bryan's contaminated food. I don't want to hear about your love lives right now."

Duncan explained, "Past lives is all we have to talk about. We've been doing the same thing for too long now."

Lauren sighed, "Not too much longer. Soon, all our time wasted will be put to good use."

"Now when you say time wasted," Fred started with Mindy kicking him from under the table. Lauren went on, "We need to get rid of these alien puppets, so we can be a more independent system."

"And be some other alien's puppet?" Jane asked while taking a drink. Duncan added, "You really buy the propaganda? We're getting funded by a different set of aliens. I don't see the new boss being any different from the old ones."

"All I know is that AIs and clones will have the rights we deserve," Lauren started getting angry. Tara patted her back, "Don't worry. We are all for the cause of synthetic liberation."

"Don't forget killing the rich!" Nick said with enthusiasm. Fred sighed, "Not all the rich and powerful suck. They are human, too."

Alisa pointed out, "People with power will always suck. It makes them self-absorbed liars and hypocrites with a lack of compassion."

"Someone paid attention in class," Alec smiled clapping his hands as did everyone else at the table. She smiled back, "I had to. I worked hard to be in school. Don't misinterpret it."

"Too late," Alec winked. Lauren laughed, "Well put. Hope we all share the same convictions in the coming struggle."

"Most of us don't have much of a choice in the matter. Yet it is an opportunity most don't get." Tara said. Jane asked, "Do tell us what you're getting at."

"Think about it. We're all up shit creek. Fred, Mindy, Bryan and Nick, all of you were about to spend years in prison. Duncan, you got screwed over in that divorce hardcore. Kathryn and Jane, well no offense, but both of you were going to be sex objects. Alisa and I had our own problems, and Alec, you were as washed up as they come," Jane revealed.

"Thank you for the history lesson wise ass. What's the point?" Nick asked still smiling. "The point is we all got second chances at life to start anew and do something different," she replied.

"By leading a violent revolution with a high likelihood of death?" Jane asked. Tara went on, "We can change things for once. We all hate how corrupt the system has gotten. Why not alter it?"

Fred pointed out, "There have been cases in history where revolutions were nonviolent. Why not take that route?"

Alec laughed, "Where's the fun in that? Everyone loves a good climax."

Duncan nudged him, "Don't you have a hard time with that?"

"Not what your ex-wife told me!" Both of them laughed, "Enjoy the sloppy seconds!"

Lauren held her head, "Juveniles."

A voice rang out, "Attention on deck!"

Everyone stood up straight as Victor said, "At ease."

Everyone sat back down looking over in his direction. He put on a speaker mic so everyone could hear him, "Hope you like what you're having. Soon we'll be experiencing the fine dining of the New Nexus Resort!"

There was a loud cheer as everyone got absorbed the news. "Our years of patience are going to pay off. The enemy has gotten lazy, fat, and complacent. They won't see what's coming. You all here are the vanguard of the coming revolution! We fight for the poor, the used and the discarded! Our time has come!" Victor shouted.

Everyone cheered again as he grabbed a keg of beer, "A pint for everyone!"

It only took five minutes for everyone to get a drink. They were ordered to wait for the toast. Once everyone was ready, Victor said, "To the future and the change that comes with it!"

They gulped down the beer and cheered soon afterwards. Bryan said, "That was some strong stuff."

Nick pointed out, "We haven't had a drink in years. We aren't going to have any tolerance to alcohol."

"Good! Less to drink in order to get drunk!" Alec slurred his lines together. Lauren smiled, "Take the rest of the night off. You've all earned it. See you tomorrow at noon."

"Sweet! We get to sleep in!" Duncan cheered. Tara grabbed Alec by the arm and told him, "Follow me."

Alec got up without hesitation and followed her. "Where are we going?" he asked.

"Trust me on this one," Tara told him as they went

down several passageways and through a door. Suddenly a set of windows over them opened up showing Jupiter in full view. "Nice."

"Right about now the massive storm should be coming into view." Tara told him. They looked as they saw the swirling red vortex travel across the gas giant. "Great view."

"It's about to get better," Tara leaped up and kissed Alec. He smiled, "Guess trust paid off for once. It's been a while."

"Same here. Let's change that," Tara told him as she started to strip. Alec stripped while kissing her over and over. Alec helped lay her down on the floor as he gave a thrust and paused. "Don't stop," Tara told him.

"I want to last. Who knows when we'll get to do this again?" Alec replied as he kissed and thrust into her again. Tara gasped as she gripped his back. Alec reached down and massaged her, "Not rusty at all!"

"Some things can't be forgotten," she whispered, "Now let's try something else." She motioned for Alec to stand up. Both of them were sweating as Tara leaped up into Alec's arms, sending him backwards into the transparent metal window. He held her tightly up as she wrapped her legs around his waist and began sliding up and down on him over and over. Tara bit into Alec's shoulder as her grip got tighter. Alec gave a wide grin as he looked up into the stars and watched everything go dark.

CHAPTER 6
REGROUP
2214
JUPITER'S ASTEROID BELT
PANDORA
INFIRMARY

"LOOKS like you were having a good dream," the doctor said as Alec woke up. His head felt numb as he sat up seeing Victor, Yosemite and Yeager. Instantly enraged, Alec leaped off of the table toward Yeager. Yosemite restrained him as Victor snapped, "Calm down!"

Alec stopped with his fists clinched and shaking. Yeager was trying not to smile. He said, "That jackass sucker punched me!"

"He's here to say sorry," Victor told Alec. This was surprising. "Really?" asked Alec.

"I'm sorry I hit you in the face and won't sucker punch you again," Yeager said it without hesitation, but it wasn't with sincerity. Victor looked back at Alec, "Well?"

Yosemite backed off. Alec walked up to Yeager and

threw a punch. He put his whole body into it, crushing Yeager's nose and knocking him down, "Apology accepted. Don't fuck with me again!"

Yeager got up resetting his nose and surprisingly keeping his cool, "Doc."

The doctor tended to his wounds. Alec looked at Victor. The once proud man now looked almost broken. His hair was completely white and his body looked skinny and frail. He told Alec sincerely, "First, I want to thank you for your help in getting me out of that shithole." There was a long pause as his eyes twitched. Victor shook it off, "So how much do you remember?"

"Wrapping up training, dinner, and Tara," Alec paused wondering where she was or if she was still alive. Victor tapped his shoulder, "At least it's started to come back no matter how painful it might be. As long as we are still alive, our work isn't over yet."

"Speaking of work, what's next?" Alec asked. Victor walked away and motioned for him to follow, "We'll see what we have left to use."

They went out the airlock and the gravity and air were activated so they could walk around the ship without airtight suits. Victor heard a noise in his ear, "Yes, Captain?"

A female's voice came over his speaker, "We've

arrived at Sparta Station, sir."

"Thank you." He went up to one of the bulkheads and tapped on it. Images of Sparta Station appeared. It was built into one of the asteroids and looked like a beehive. Victor sighed, "You'll be hearing soon how far we have to go to get out of the proverbial creek we are in. At least we're going not going to be without a paddle. I'll be checking up on you from time to time. Go to your briefing."

Victor and Yosemite walked off down the passageway as Yeager come up behind Alec, "Follow me."

He cautiously followed, keeping his guard up. He led him back to the same classroom as before. Everyone seemed to be in the same spots as before as well. Kathryn asked, "Are we going to have any more issues with you two trying to kill each other?"

Yeager went first with a quick, "No."

"If he doesn't mess with me, I won't mess with him. That's all I'm promising," Alec told her taking a seat. Kathryn nodded her head, "Good enough. We've got enough problems to worry about."

She brought up images of what they had left. It wasn't much. "I'll try to make this as quick as possible, but it's bad. The Pandora is the last capital ship we have left, our infiltrator ships have all been destroyed, Sparta Station

One is our last stronghold, and only four destroyers and three frigates are remaining. We only have two hundred fighters, and our ground teams are barely at battalion strength. It's only a matter of time before Sparta Station One is discovered, so everything that can be transferred is being sent to Pandora. Any questions before we move on?" Kathryn informed the group.

Mira asked, "What's plan B?"

Kathryn went on, "I just got done with a meeting with the higher ups. To put it bluntly, we're running."

"Shit, really?" Cullen said standing up. Jane tried to recommend, "We could go guerilla again and start from square one."

"I said the same thing, but the commanders don't think so." Kathryn explained as Yeager snapped, "Lost their nerves have they?"

"I wouldn't go so far to say that. They are going with Yosemite's decision to go after the supporting organizations of the Alliance instead of the Alliance itself." Kathryn told us. Alec raised his hand, "So we're going after the Vegans?"

"Yes. We are going to fucking tear that empire down. First we need to get out of this system. If you'd please." Kathryn motioned to the screen. She brought up images of the plan, "Phase one, we are going to get a 'faster than light' engine on this ship. Phase two, we need to cut off all communications and contact between the Alliance and the Vegans. Phase three, we go to Vegan space and bring their government to an early end. Once that is over, we come back, grind and win! We haven't lost yet, and we're not giving up."

"So what could I remember that could possibly change this situation we're in?" Alec asked wondering if that would help. "They think you saw something that could hurt the Vegans. I don't know the specifics, but I guess we'll find out soon with the way you're recovering. For now, get some rest. We've been working our asses off this week and could use a break. I'll call everyone back here when something else comes up."

Alec followed everyone out the airlock as they went up to the mess deck. Unlike the massive one on the station, this one was more compact. The overhead was lower, seats were attached to the table and the food was stuck in plastic bags. Everyone took seats at the same wooden table and started squeezing the food out of the bags. It was okay, yet on the bland side. Alec was glad he didn't have to eat to survive. Everyone seemed quiet as they slowly ate the pasty substance. Alec asked, "So how is it that aliens can travel across the galaxy without a faster than light drive?"

Jane explained, "Artificial wormholes. There is a

network of them spread out thought this galaxy keeping everyone connected. From what we could gather, there was some kind of conflict years ago that lead to a treaty that banned alternate means of space travel besides the wormholes."

"Why's that?" Alec asked puzzled by the information. Kathryn went on, "They thought it would prevent another major war from happening. It worked. Only downside is that it led the two major powers, the Stallions and Vegans, to use the less developed races as proxies to fight one another."

It started to click in Alec's head, "Guess I see why they want to use us to do their dirty work and break the rules. If anything would go wrong, they could deny any involvement."

Cullen looked at me with dismay in his eyes, "Thanks for bringing that up, seeing how we are getting left to rot after things went wrong."

"Forgive me if I seem insensitive to our plight, but maybe knowing how things went wrong could help us out. So how did things go wrong?" Alec pressed the issue more concerned about his curiosity than empathy. Yeager told him, "We've told you! Squadron Thirteen, your squadron, fucked up! We don't know exactly how you guys screwed up, but there was only one person that made it out alive."

"I got it. It was me." Alec regretted asking the question. Yeager leaned back in his seat, "In a manner of speaking."

"Okay… so in my memories, I didn't see most of you. Why is that?" Alec probed for more information. Mira told him, "I'm positive you'll found out more in your next flashback, so stop bugging us about the past! We've got bigger problems here and…!" Before she could finish the ship violently rocked and a loud thud echoed through the ship. Alarms went off soon after and the lights turned red. A voice came over the intercom, "General quarters, general quarters! Set conduction Zebra throughout the ship. This is not a drill. All hands, don protective gear and man your battle stations! All non-essential personnel, stand by to repel boarders."

When they heard that, they all reached down and put on breathing devices as the air got siphoned out. The temperature dropped as the internal heating units were shut off. They got to the airlock just as the gravity was being shut down and the lights were being turned off. The six of them packed into the small space before exiting on the other side. Over the intercom a voice spoke out, "Conduction Zebra set."

Several other crewmen were going in specified directions depending on where their station was. Alec and the others headed to the center of the ship where the armory and most other vital parts of the ship were located. That way, the main control rooms could be defended with the small arms stored nearby. They grabbed onto a revolving line that sped up the time it would take them to move. It almost felt like flying as they were dragged though the passageways. Alec suddenly had a set of arms grabbing him as he and everyone else was thrown into the armory. Inside were several lockers filled with weapons, ammo, and armored suits. At the door were four armed guards checking everyone that was coming in. Thankfully it was enough room to move around. Alec went over to his locker and put on his armored suit as quickly as possible. The alarms finally stopped and a female's voice came over the intercom, "This is the Captain. The Alliance has discovered our location and are closing in with eighteen ships and another twenty on the way. We'll be using Jupiter to slingshot us out of the area. The Alliance thinks they can take this ship as a trophy. Let's show them otherwise. Captain out."

Once Alec was fully geared up, Kathryn motioned for him to follow her. He kicked his feet against the locker and flew out the exit door back into the hallway. They had to use the groves in the walls to move through the passageway. Each of them bounced side to side, gaining momentum. They had to pile in and out of airlocks three times before they got to their position. Alec heard, "Infiltration pods incoming!"

When they got to the location displayed in their eyes, the airlock behind them closed, leaving them cut off from the rest of the ship. There were grooves for the team to take cover behind inside the passageway. They peeked out while aiming at the door as they settled into the grooves. Kathryn told the team, "Remember, we're in zero gravity. Don't get a puncture in your suits. Use the laws of physics while fighting. Brace for flash bangs and grenades!"

Thinking about physics, Alec propped himself against the bulkhead with his legs, holding his back against the opposite side. The red light shut off completely and the night vision automatically activated. They waited there as the ship rocked periodically. Alec stared down the octagon shaped passageway waiting for the door to open, his weapon at the ready. The aim point moved only slightly. They waited and waited. Alec had to ask, "How long is it going to be before they try boarding? In fact, why are they trying to board?"

Cullen snapped, "Really? Could you stop asking so many damned questions already! I understand you have amnesia, but seriously! They'll fucking come when they can break through our energy shields, weapons systems, armor plating, and fighters. That's when they'll come! All we need to worry about is wasting the bastards if they do!"

A loud thud sent everyone forward suddenly as they saw the hull buckle. Quickly everyone got back into position as sparks started flying out the door. Kathryn yelled, "That was a little too quick. Well, let's welcome them aboard!"

The door was split open without a sound. Tara got off a grenade round right through the open door as several grenades headed back towards them. Alec ducked into the corner as they started going off. None of them emitted any noise as the spheres of light flashed nearby. He felt like someone was hitting him over the head with every shockwave. His energy shields went out leaving him with only the armor to protect himself. The temperature seemed to rise and fall after every blast. The explosions stopped as suddenly as they began.

Alec suddenly saw an armored soldier with a human face mask pointing a rifle at him. Alec reached forward, swiping his barrel out of the way just in time as a shot was fired and missed him. Alec held down the trigger to his own weapon while the soldier went the opposite way. The dead body went back into his comrades. They shoved forward as they fired away. Alec's shields recharged just in time as he took a hit from a plasma shotgun. He slammed into the bulkhead and bounced off, losing his grip on his weapon. Quickly he pulled out a plasma pistol, leaped over and started grappling with a soldier for his shotgun. Alec pushed the soldier into his friend and shot them both while flying backwards.

Yeager got into a grappling match with one of the Alliance operatives. Both of them fought for control of a rifle as they shoved each other into the opposite bulkhead. Mira got one of her arms shot off by a plasma blast. She let out a scream, and Cullen grabbed Mira to pull her to safety, losing a leg in the process. A plasma round hit him right as he got to the back of the craft, burning through his armor, flesh and bone. Thankfully both their wounds were cauterized by the heat from the rounds. Kathryn took a direct hit to the torso. Her shields went out in a flash and she went flying down towards Alec. Jane was left alone holding the Alliance soldiers at the door by rapidly firing away at the entrance.

Alec bounced back against the bulkhead and flew back towards the door, past the bodies and limbs. He grabbed a rifle and jabbed the barrel into the gut of an Alliance soldier so hard, the barrel went through his armor and into his belly. Alec propped his legs against the bulkhead and fired. The plasma round burned through the soldier's body and impacted into another operative. He fired again, hitting the man Yeager was grappling with. This gave Yeager the chance to go for his knife and cut the other man's throat. The two of them pushed the dead bodies and limbs into the air lock slowing down their advance. Kathryn yelled in a distorted voice, "Frag them!"

Yeager and Jane threw grenades into the doorway exploding the pod. It was blown off the ship and sent flying away. Alec leaped back up towards the door looking outside. The Alliance ships looked like giant d-shaped oval disks. The Spartan's destroyers looked like black three tipped stars, while their frigates were shaped like large black triangles. Both sets of ships could move in any direction and fire away at each other with missiles, phase blasts, and plasma torpedoes. When a ship would explode, it would go out in a sphere of flame sending the debris in every direction. The Spartans rigged several asteroids and used them to attack the Alliance. One capital ship was ripped right in half.

Among the metal hull plates, flying sparks, and venting air, there were hundreds of people floating helplessly into oblivion. They vanished in the resulting explosion in a blink of an eye. Two groups of fighters seemed to by flying backwards firing away at each other. The Spartan's Hawk fighters looked like flat triangles, and the Alliance's Eagles looked like flying cylinders with wings. They peppered each other with plasma rounds over and over. Whoever's shields went out first would lose. For being out numbered and out gunned, the Spartans were holding their own. Suddenly more Alliance ships came from below. A voice cried, "Brace for shock!"

Suddenly Alec was sent flying backwards again as the ship was rocked. He slammed against the airlock going right back to the door. He stopped himself from moving by grabbing onto a loss overhead panel. He saw an Alliance ship get its hull blasted apart outside. The heat from the lasers cut the metal alloy like butter. A single red torpedo went crashing into the ship. The vessel veered off showing off several other hits she'd taken. The resulting explosion reminded Alec of a glass plate hitting a floor and shattering. The ball of fire exploded out towards them. Kathryn yelled again, "Get the door closed!"

Yeager and Alec both pushed on opposite sides closing the door just in time. The shockwave knocked them around again. Yeager slammed his head into a wall panel with such force that he got knocked out. Alec spiraled around the passageway helpless to stop himself. Jane grabbed Alec and pulled him to the side. Both of them held on as the ship violently rocked over and over again. The constant loud thuds didn't let up. The two of them held position in the passageway holding each other tight. She cried, "Tell me everything's going to be okay!"

"It will be," Alec reassured her as he clutched her close. They got pinned against one another because of the way the ship was moving. "We must have been making our slingshot around Jupiter," Alec thought. He reached forward and activated a monitor. Alec brought up an image of the ship's turn around Jupiter and motioned Jane to look, too. She started calming down. Alec turned off his night vision, seeing only space and the reflection off of Jane's helmet. The ship made its turnaround Jupiter as Alec and Jane felt another jolt. The ship gained speed and momentum as it went along. Alec shifted the view to where Sparta Station was. There was only now a giant ball of fire and a shower of small rocks where it used to stand. The way the rocks burned in Jupiter's atmosphere as they came raining down looked like shooting stars on a clear night. "Everything is going to be okay," Alec said again.

Jupiter again encompassed their whole view as the Pandora flew past the massive planet. Alec and Jane stared in awe as the gas clouds moved around the atmosphere. Both of them grasped their hands together as things literally felt like they were getting hotter. The Pandora now had to escape orbit. She gave everything her engine had to avoid falling into the gas giant. Jupiter started to get smaller as the Pandora started to increases its distance. Both Alec and Jane breathed a sigh of relief as the planet got smaller and smaller in their view. They kept holding each other as both of them felt comfortable enough to sleep. Alec could feel Jane's body breathe as her chest rose up and down on his chest. Alec's eyes got heavy as he leaned back and let them close.

CHAPTER 7
UPRISING
2209
ORBIT OF MARS
NEW NEXUS
HOTEL ROOM

"COME on Alec. Wake up!" Tara tapped on Alec's arm.

He moaned as he woke up, but quickly smiled when he saw here. "Why hello."

"It's too early for that." She threw him his clothing, and they both started to get dressed. The hotel room they were in was nice, the best bed they slept on in some time. The images of space around them made the room feel bigger than it was. Alec asked, "No, it's not. We can't have a quickie?"

Tara laughed, "Tell you what, when we're done taking over this place, we can have a victory after party. Sound good?"

Alec finished putting on his shoes, "Sounds worth it."

The two of them walked out of the room and went down the hallways of red doors on each side of them. They got to the elevator and took it down. After that they came out to the sound of music, slot machines, and cheers. There were rows upon rows of slot machines with different holographic animations. There were also live dancers on random dance platforms. Most of them were dressed erotically. The bartenders juggled around their drinks as they served them, putting on a show. The booze was flowing just like the currency. There were always well dressed employees going around giving out drinks to loosen wallets and minds alike. Smoke machines were also readily available, offering different types of tobacco, weed, opiates, or hookah, depending on what the customer wanted. The restaurants had a wide range of Earth food for the taking. Last but not least, the oldest profession in the world was still running strong here with androids offering a good time for the lonely. In every direction people walked around going to their next selection of indulgence. Alec smiled getting a feeling of nostalgia as he walked along with Tara, "This brings me back. So where are we meeting?"

She pointed to a coffee shop where the others waved for them to come over. The two of them took a seat with drinks already there waiting for them. Duncan nudged Alec, "Couldn't get out of the room slow enough, could you?"

"Not the room, bed on the other hand…" Alec winked with Tara playfully kicking him in the leg. Bryan cried as he spilled his coffee, "Stupid cup!"

Fred asked, "Are we really taking him with us on this caper? He might drop something more vital next time."

"Just focus on what you need to do to not drop anything. Your hands are already shaking from the caffeine," Mandy told him as he tried to stop twitching. Nick patted him on the back, "Should have smoked some weed. This cinnamon bun is delicious."

"Is he fucking high?" Jane 68 asked looking concerned as he overly enjoyed his pastry. Tara motioned over to Alisa who was drinking a lot of water, "Could be hung over."

"Fucking snitch!" Alisa snapped. Lauren quietly yelled, "We can still smell the booze on you! Shit, what part of don't get hammered didn't you understand?"

"I'll be fine. I stopped drinking at midnight. I threw up already and took some pills," Alisa tried to reassure her. Lauren rolled her eyes pulling out pills of her own, "I knew one or two of you bastards would overdo it. Glad I came prepared."

She handed a pill to Alisa and Nick. Both of them quickly consumed the pills feeling different moments after. Nick sat up straight, "My buzz is gone!"

"The ringing stopped!" Alisa smiled able to lift her head again. Fred asked in dismay, "Wait, you had recovery pills all along? Way to hold out on us. I wanted to get drunk, too!"

Lauren handed Duncan a pill as well. He sighed, "What gave me a way?"

"Nothing. I just knew you would." She smiled. Nick shock his head side to side, "I should have done more!"

"Tell you what, I'll get you something when this is over," she told him. Bryan asked, "If this is 'fleet week' here then where are the sailors?"

Alec sighed and explained, "They are in civilian attire. Really think they would party in a place like this in dress uniform?"

"Don't worry. We know who's who here. We got this. All of us, right?" Mindy looked around at the team as each off them nodded their heads. Mindy said with a little nervousness, "Almost thought this day would never come."

"It's been coming for some time. Best indication of that is the calm before the storm," Lauren explained as Jane 69 came up to the table in a skimpy green waitress outfit showing off her curves, "Here's that refill you've been asking for."

She handed Lauren a cup along with key cards and combinations as well. "Thank you."

Jane walked off tending to other customers. Her sister smiled, "Glad I wasn't the one to bus tables."

"Luck of the draw. Had to have people on the inside. Makes life so much easier," Lauren grinned as she enjoyed her drink. Jane suddenly came back to the table with a look of worry on her face, "I forgot your reset."

Lauren took it, "Really? I thought..." She paused when she looked at the holographic image displayed to her. "I got to go. Stay here. Don't leave until I get back!"

She got up and followed Jane off into the crowd. The rest of the team sat there wondering what was going on. Alec got up with Tara grabbing his arm, "She said stay here."

"I don't like being left in the dark. I'll be back." Alec left the table with the others giving looks of protest as they moved through the crowd. He kept track of them following Jane's sparkling green outfit. The two of them went into a door off in the background with Alec following unnoticed. They got to a small locker room off the beaten path. Alec stayed outside and listened in as best he could. Lauren started off, "Kathryn? I just want to talk. Please tell me what's wrong?"

"This shouldn't be happening!" Kathryn said sounding like she was terrified. Lauren kept pressing, "Well we are about to make history. Is that freaking you out, or is there something else?"

There was a thud on the floor that sounded like a plastic object bouncing off the ceramic floor. Jane suddenly gasped, "Did you use this?"

"Don't be coy. What the hell is that thing supposed to do?" Lauren asked getting impatient with the situation. Kathryn sighed, "Pregnancy test…"

"What?" Alec let out uncontrollably, loud enough to where Lauren heard it. She reached out the door, grabbed him and pulled him in. He got slammed down on the floor with Lauren on top of him, "What part of 'don't leave the table' did you not understand?"

"I thought this had to do with the mission…" Alec muttered as someone else walked in. It was just some random woman who froze staring at us. Lauren snapped, "Do you mind! We're trying go fuck here!"

She went down and started kissing Alec over and over making the woman leave. Once she was gone, Lauren put her knee on Alec's groin and applied pressure with him gasping. "What didn't you understand?"

"Sorry! Please stop!" Alec begged. Lauren pushed

his head into the floor as she got up walking in circles. He had to ask, "How did Kathryn get pregnant? I mean, congratulations!"

Jane asked while holding her head, "Still a good question, how did she… well…"

"According to prude ancient people, they said storks drop of babies," Lauren said sarcastically. Jane sighed, "I don't think that tall tale applies to androids."

"Was she specially built?" Alec asked innocently enough. Lauren almost grinded her teeth saying, "We're built and designed by lonely perverted nerds! What do you think?"

"Pregnancy fetish?" Alec's guess only enraged Lauren even more. Kathryn cried, "It was a fucking nerd stalker that did this to me! I was just trying to maintain cover! He knew my name. I got him to shut up by…"

"Still leaves more questions than answers," Alec said with Lauren kicking him in the gut. She snapped, "Out of all the times! Out of all the places! This isn't going to fuck up years of planning! Kathryn, if you don't feel up to…"

She stood up wiping off the tears, "I'll carry on! Nothing has changed."

"Good. Everyone back to work!" Lauren reached down and picked Alec up and pushed him through the door. Before they entered back into the crowd, she told him while grabbing his crotch and applying pressure, "Not a word of this!"

"Okay! Please stop!" She pulled Alec back to the table and she motioned for everyone else to follow. Everyone followed Lauren discreetly as possible blending in with the crowd as best they could. They regrouped on the terminal section of the station where all the ships were moored up. There was a clear view of them through the station's transparent metal windows. There were rows of the oval shaped black colored ships encompassed in a cage that kept them in place. There was only one way on and off each ship and that was through a cylindrical tube that connected to the ship's airlock. This section of the station was almost empty with no major arrivals and departures in the area. Lauren went to a locker and started pulling out duffel bags for each of them to grab. One by one, they went up and grabbed one of a different color and kept on going. Nobody in the terminal seemed to pay much attention to them. The security guards seemed to be mindlessly strolling around the area.

They came up on a security checkpoint where they were waved though without question. One of the security personnel at the checkpoint gave a wink to them. Must have been in on the plan. So far, so good. They made it to the entrance corridor to the ship that was selected for them to board. There were only two crew men manning a watch standing in their way. They went into a nearby bathroom and closed the door once they were all in. All of them open their bags pulling out their gear and grabbing their weapons. Their load out was simple: just a vest to hold ammo, half of them armed with SMG's and the other with shotguns (lethal and non-lethal rounds) attached to lanyards keeping them on their bodies, plasma pistol, holster, communicators, glasses with computers built in, and an experimental device.

Lauren went over the plan one last time. She looked at each of them, "Remember your training, and this will be easy. Most of the crew is off partying and the few crewmembers that are on board will more than likely be nursing hangovers. Most of the watch standards will not be armed. Use non-lethal ammo first. They are quieter and will not set off any alarms. Hit them hard, and fast and they won't put up much of a fight. Only go lethal as a last resort. We want them to coward out, not fight to the death. Now what is our job?"

All of them said together, "Pave the way."

"Damn straight. Keep the doors open for the follow on teams and then?" Lauren asked. "Secure the main armory," all of them said together again. Lauren nodded giving a slight smile, "Let's go."

She leaned out the door throwing a holo-decoy in front of the two watch standards. It kept their attention as the main team and follow on group quietly walked up to them. They stayed right up against the window on the balls of their feet. All of them were in a single file line with their weapons pointed down at the deck not flagging any of their comrades. Alec was right behind Lauren as they got closer and closer. One of the guards turned slightly seeing a row of a hundred people armed to the teeth right next to them. All she could utter out was, "Oh shit!"

Both Alec and Lauren threw stun darts that knocked them out instantly. Fred and Mindy ran over grabbing them before they could hit the deck and gently laid them down. Lauren got to the corner and peeked out before making the turn. For taking long strides they didn't make any noise as they went down the corridor towards the ship itself. They passed by a holographic sign that said, "Welcome to Alliance Interstellar Ship Caesar."

Lauren signaled everyone to pause making everyone come to a stop. She grabbed out a stun grenade and counted down to three with the explosive in hand. Alec crouched down getting ready to make a sprint. Once all her fingers were back on the grenade, Alec, Duncan, Fred, Alisa, and Mindy went beside Lauren as she lobbed the grenade into the ship. The six of them made a dash while staying in a straight line running for the entrance. They saw the rectangular shaped air lock with both doors open. Behind that was a quarter deck complete with a podium and two blinded watch standards holding their eyes. Fred and Mindy leaped forwards putting hydraulic clamps on the doors to keep them from closing while Duncan and Alisa shot stun rounds into the watch standard. Lauren and Alec swept the rest of the area for personnel checking each corner. Lauren said, "Clear!"

Alec replied, "All clear!"

The quarter deck had two octagon passageways going in opposite directions wide enough for two people to walk side by side. Twenty people gathered on the quarter deck and headed in opposite directions soon followed by many others, each with their own area of the ship to clear. Team Thirteen had an important one with the armory. Alec and Lauren took point walking side by side down the passage way with the others following them. With every door and hatch that came along, they covered with their weapons' muzzles, making sure they didn't get suppressed. They got to a ladder well on their left. Lauren halted them and took a quick peek while aiming with her weapon.

Alec came around to the other side as they went

down the ladder well. Alec turned to his right when he got down the stairs covering a door and a hatch as the rest of the team climbed down. Bryan tapped his shoulder as they turned around heading to the armory door with Tara on the opposite side waiting. Alec aimed with his shotgun at the lock on the outside. Tara positioned her hand nearby to open the door after the lock was shot off. With a loud bang the lock was shattered in a bright flash of light as Tara pulled the door open. Alec went forward aiming his shotgun inside suppressing the two occupants inside. Alisa got next to him almost losing her aim as she started laughing. The armory guard and a female crewmate were in each other's arms naked looking pale as a ghost staring at them. Alec smiled, "What a dereliction of duty, letting yourselves get caught with your pants down both literally and metaphorically."

"If you want we can let you two wrap up out in the passageway, just not in there. Get out! Don't bother covering yourself, and keep your hands up!" Alisa motioned for them to leave. The two of them still held each other as they slid out of the armory and into the passageway. Mindy and Fred kept them covered. Alec went inside the armory, "Clear."

"All clear." Lauren grabbed the two sets of blue coveralls and held them up to the terrified crewmembers.

She explained, "I'll make you two a deal. Answer my questions, and I'll let you two put these uniforms back on and leave with your lives and bodies intact. If you two feel like being heroes, I'm positive you could use your imagination on what pain we can inflict. So tell us how many watch standers are currently armed and how many crewmembers have keys to the magazines and ready lockers? Save us the trouble of checking the logs."

Bryan and Jane both shouted, "Freeze! Don't fucking move!"

There was a sudden sound of crying from a person trying to climb the ladder well out of a birthing. Nick walked over, "Oh come on! These two people got caught butt fucking naked, and they still have more dignity than you do!"

Jane smelled the air, "Did you crap yourself?"

The man couldn't respond as he kept sobbing uncontrollably unable to move. Bryan sighed, "Please stop. This is just getting depressing."

He couldn't. Mindy looked over and said, "Is there anyone else down there? Are you now pissing yourself?"

Tara kept on laughing as Alisa remarked, "This guy's going places. He's still standing tall if you know what I mean."

Lauren sighed, "Really? We're taking over a ship

and you're looking at someone's… okay. I'll give you props, way to keep your composure unlike crybaby over there."

"Thanks. The officer of the deck is armed along with the rover and combined system maintenance center watch standard. The duty section officer and duty section chief have keys to the backup armory and ready locker," he told them while trying to shield the woman. Lauren stepped in front of him, "Really?"

Alec looked at the log and handed them both their coveralls. "He's telling the truth. I'm sending the information to the other teams. He just saved both of your asses. Seeing how fear is still keeping him energized you two can finish each other off in the hotel. Everyone is happy and alive. Might have been caught with your pants down, but at least you both still have your dignity…unlike sissy boy down there."

Bryan lost his patience, "Okay weeper. Let's go."

He took a couple steps down pulling the man up the ladder well when he was grabbed and pulled down the stairs. Both Fred and Mindy charged after him knocking the crying man out of the way. There was a lot of shouting and a couple rounds went off. After the rounds went off the crying man passed out falling on his face. There seemed to be an eternity of quiet until the words, "Clear" and "All Clear" were said.

Nick and Jane carried two knocked out crewmembers up the ladder well and Mindy and Lauren carried Bryan up as he held his belly. Tara sighed, "Figures he would get hurt."

A third man came up followed by Duncan as he kept jabbing his SMG muzzle into the man's back, "Fuck off!"

Alisa walked over and grabbed his throat giving it a squeeze. Lauren had to pull her off before she chocked him too much. As the man gasped for air, Lauren commanded, "Easy! Everyone calm the fuck down. Don't push your luck! Each of you pick up one of your passed out comrades!"

The three awake members of the crew picked them up and waited. Lauren went around and put zip ties around their arms securing them to their unconscious friends. The armorer told them, "There's a secondary infirmary through that door to the left, red cross, can't miss it."

"Thanks you. You've been a cool customer. For that, Duncan and Alisa, escort them off the ship. Stick to stun. They've been mostly cooperative. Congratulations. You all get to live. Don't take this the wrong way, but I hope we don't meet again."

"No offense taken," the armory guard said. Duncan went up the ladder well first and one by one the crewmembers went up. After Alisa went up, Lauren ordered, "Tara and Nick, hold down the armory. Mindy and Fred, grab Bryan's legs. Alec, lead the way. Alec went ahead through the open door and peered around the corner. He motioned for the rest of the team to follow. Alec saw the red cross and busted the door open. Mindy and Fred placed Bryan on the surgical table as he moaned. Mindy pulled off Bryan's vest and ripped his shirt off showing a knife wound to the belly button on his right side. Fred started gagging and went back out into the passageway vomiting. "Really?" asked Alec.

"Sorry. Blood makes me sick" he whimpered. Alec sighed, "At least you're not acting like that one guy."

"Yeah, what a wimp." He vomited again, "Okay, I'm good!"

"I'm not, asshole!" Bryan cried as Mindy grabbed out several medical tools. "This is going to hurt," she warned.

"I'm already in pain! Just do something!" Bryan snapped as Mindy got to work. She injected medical gel into the wound making a sizzling sound as it stopped the bleeding and clotted the wound. "This is going to hurt more."

She went down with a tissue regenerator that moved like a sewing machine across his belly as he cried in pain. It took a minute to finish going across the wound. Lauren grabbed some towels and wiped away the blood from the wound, "So what did we learn from this?"

"Always check a space before going into it." Bryan moaned in shame and pain as he wiped way the tears. Mindy wrapped gauze around the wound, "You should be able to walk. Just don't make too many sudden movements, or you'll undo the work I just did."

Lauren reported over the radio, "Team lead, Squad Thirteen lead; main armory is secured."

A voice came over, "Squad Thirteen lead, team one lead; ship is secure. All teams stand down. Once relived by our crew or this ship, gather up on the mess decks."

"Team lead, Squad Thirteen lead out." Lauren breathed a sigh of relief as she leaned up against the bulkhead. Nick asked, "So how did we do?"

"None of you swept each other with your weapons. You kept your chicken wings close to your bodies, kept your bodies squared, and we only suffered one cut wound," she looked over and Bryan as he looked away embarrassed. Fred handed him a shirt. "All and all at least we didn't screw up."

Nick asked, "What do you mean by that?"

Lauren explained as she let her SMG hang off her lanyard taking a set. "Out of the eight ships docked, one got away…"

"What?" Everyone said at once. Tara asked, "Shouldn't we go after it?"

"No need. It took a couple hits on the way out. It won't be able to communicate, nor will it be able to get to where we're heading before us. Like I said earlier, just worry about what we have to do to get the job done." She told them as Duncan and Alisa came back down the ladder well. They held five cans of beer each. Duncan laughed, "I had a feeling that you would pull though."

Bryan smiled as he caught a beer after it had gotten thrown to him. Alisa explained, "Looted the storage room on the way back. Team lead said it was good for us to have just one."

"Fine by me," Lauren grabbed a drink and waited for everyone to get one themselves. She looked around and smiled opening the drink. Bryan's almost exploded on him, "It's still good!"

"Might have been sloppy, but we all made it. Let's enjoy it while it lasts. To loot and glory!" Lauren held up the metal can as did everyone else before taking a swig. Jane laughed, "They might have been poor defenders, but they have good taste in drinks."

Tara asked, "So what's next?"

"The Pettit Space Station and Elevator." Lauren

paused taking another swig of her drink. The others looked on quietly. Duncan said, "So we're going home at last."

"Yeah. Should be one hell of a homecoming." She finished her drink and threw the can aside, "Come Bryan, we're going to the debriefing. The rest of you can rest."

"Why me? Never mind. I'll go." Bryan finished his drink and followed Lauren up the ladder well. Tara grabbed Alec and pulled him into the armory, "So about that victory party…"

The two of them started kissing. The others went down to the birthing with Mindy sighing, "We stole it, and now we must clean it."

Over the intercom a voice said, "All hands, make preparations for getting underway."

Alec laughed as he took off his vest, "This vessel isn't the only one getting started."

"Good to hear." Tara and Alec kissed passionately as the ship hummed to life with all the systems being activated. There was a loud clank as the ship detached from the dock. "Under way."

"So are we!" Tara leaped on Alec as he went to full speed himself.

CHAPTER 8
2214
RECON
SOL SYSTEM'S ASTEROID BELT
PANDORA
AIRLOCK PASSAGE WAY

A lec woke up when the gravity was reactivated. Jane was still in his arms and fell into his lap. The doors behind them opened up with medical personnel running in to attend to the wounded. Right next to them, Alec saw the face of a woman seemingly looking up at him. She had on Alliance battle gear and a wound on her neck. When covered head to toe in armored suits, it was hard to tell genders apart, especially in the heat of a fight when said people are trying to kill each other. The deck was covered in dead bodies and severed limbs. There was blood all over the bulkheads from it floating around in the low gravity environment. Jane asked, "We're alive?"

"As much as we'll ever be," Alec replied as he helped her up. He saw Yeager push away the medics and snap, "I'm fine!"

Cullen limped past with the help of a medic as he carried his severed leg with him. Mira had to be carried out on a stretcher as she cried, "Why is my arm itching? It's not attached!"

A couple of crewmen came in and started pilling the dead Alliance soldiers in the airlock. Kathryn was also being carried out on a stretcher. Surprisingly, she was still functional. Yeager went up to her and grabbed her hand, "Are you all right?"

"I'm fine. I'm going to need you all to carry on for me while I recover, okay?" Kathryn told him. He nodded, "Okay. Just get better. I would hate to lose you."

"I know you would." She looked up at Jane, "Take care while I recuperate. You'll get briefed on your next mission in the training room."

She got carried off by the medics as the last of the dead Alliance soldiers got put inside the airlock. The door closed suddenly and the other opened. Their bodies vented out into space. As the crewmen started wiping off the blood, Jane left Alec's arms and stood by herself. Her helmet folded back into her suit and she said, "No point standing around; we got a job to do."

She motioned for us to follow her. I looked over at Yeager, "So you and Kathryn are close?"

He shook his head side to side, grinding his teeth. With his knuckles popping he said, "I can't wait for your ignorance to be lifted."

Alec backed off not waiting to start anything. As they went down the passageway, the crewmembers were repairing the damage from the last fight. Some were replacing panels, others were fixing wiring, but most were just cleaning. The air felt stale as it had been recycled from earlier. Once again, they were back in the same classroom as before. It felt a lot emptier this time being that there were only three of them now. It wasn't long before Victor's face appeared in a holographic projection, "Greetings, I'll keep this short as I can. Most of what we had left was able to escape Jupiter, but there was some sacrifice involved. I hate to do this, but no rest for the weary. We need you three to go on a reconnaissance mission. Only recon, avoid fighting if possible. Additional mission details and equipment will be provided in the transport that has been assigned for your use. Good luck."

The hologram went off, and the lights came back on. Jane sighed, "Let's see what's out there."

The three of them went back out the airlock and headed for the hanger bay. It didn't take long for them to get there. Inside were several rectangular fighters and transports all undergoing repairs. There were spare parts laying around in random piles, dead bodies being thrown into space along with the other wreckage that wasn't needed on board. Alec got a closer look at the space craft seeing them in better detail. The fighters were a long thin triangle shape named Hawk. Most of their weapons were tucked inside the craft itself. The transports, or drop ships, were called Crains. They might have been armed, but they weren't as nimble as the fighters were. They were wide and short. All of the small craft were painted black in order to blend in with the background of space just like the ships themselves. The docks for each craft reminded him of a beehive with a cove for each vehicle. In front of the three, a mechanic walked up, "We're short on pilots and AI's right now. Can any of you fly?"

Jane stepped up, "I can."

"Good, that will be your bird." He pointed over to the only Crain that looked like it was still functional. Jane led the way as the other two followed her up to the Crain. In the back there was a ladder for them to climb in. The inside looked familiar with the seats on the sides and equipment racks in the center. The transport air vented into the storage compartments leaving the inside of the craft empty of air. There were no gravity controls either leaving them to floating around inside. At the end of the storage area was the cockpit where the Crain was piloted from. The three of them all took seats and strapped inside the cockpit. The holographic controls came online eliminating the compartment. Like the bigger ships, there were no external windows to see out of, only cameras to trust as visual aids.

On the main console was a three dimensional compass showing a three access grid, a three dimensional map of the area around them, the transport's location, fuel, ammo, weapons, shield, hull integrative, fuel, ammo and shield integrity as well. There was a double handled joystick with holographic images of a cube. Depending on where the center of the stick was, indicated by a round blue ball against an orange glowing cube, the craft would either head up, down, forwards, backwards, side to side or diagonally. The further the ball got away from the center of the cube, the faster the ship would go. Alec could rotate the grips all the way around to flip the transport over. There were four foot pedals to adjust the axis that the craft traveled as well. The weapons were located on the long sides of the ship, and the engines were in the corners of the craft. The Hawks had a similar design but more guns and speed, yet no payload. Jane got on the controls and asked over the radio, "Pandora tower, this is Crain Twenty Two. Request permission to take off."

"Twenty two, tower, permission granted. Stay on

designated flight path until outside of immediate area," the controller told her. She replied, "Tower, twenty two; copy out."

There was a sudden jolt as the docking clamps released and the transport free floated in the bay. The door in front of them opened up showing the void of space as the Crain slowly flew outside the ship. Jane set the controls for autopilot as they moved the cameras around to take a look at the damage. The Pandora had several hull breaches being repaired using the asteroids nearby for materials. Three of the four destroyers made it, but only one of the three frigates did. Each of them huddled around Pandora's five point star shape structure getting needed repairs. They looked like a school of fish swimming together. The fighters were flying patrols nearby and the transports were being used to assist in repairs. Jane switched the screen back to the Crain's course and leaned back in the pilot's seat. She grabbed a data pad that was hanging on the overhead and started reading to herself. Yeager interrupted, "Well don't leave us hanging. What's the job?"

"Intel suspects that there is a deposit of..." She looked at the text, "...code named Icarus partial on a nearby asteroid that's currently being mined. All we need to do is scout out the area, see if said element is there and also see what kind of security they have," Jane explained throwing the pad away. "That's it."

"How long is it going to take for us to get there?" Yeager asked while taking some pills. Jane thought about it, "At this speed, we'll be at the first checkpoint in ten minutes, and then we'll go on silent running. That will add another five hours until we get to our destination."

Yeager sighed grabbing his head as he leaned back in his seat. Alec asked, "So know any good ways to kill time?"

"Stabbing is a good one," Yeager said looking at him. Alec was tired of the threats, "Well, seeing how we got time, what the hell is your issue with me? And what was ignorance stuff you were talking about earlier?"

Yeager got up and headed for the door, "I agreed not to kill you. That doesn't mean we're talking. I'll be in back sleeping. I need rest after getting knocked out."

The door closed leaving Jane and Alec alone. He shook his head side to side, "What a jerk."

Jane sighed, "I don't get it. I thought you both got along just fine. Guess he doesn't like the fact you don't remember."

"Come on! It's coming back to me! I remember the New Nexus hijackings," Alec tried to explain still feeling frustrated. He then thought about it, "Hey, how did Kathryn get pregnant anyway?"

Jane laughed, "I haven't thought about that is some time. Best way it could be explained is a design flaw. No one really talked about it."

"What happened to the child?" Jane looked back at the door, "You were just looking at him. Yeager is said child."

"What? How's that possible? He's only five? That doesn't add up!" Alec wondered about it as Jane laughed, "What can you say? He's a freak just like the rest of us."

"Now when you say freak, do you mean of nature or of…" She interrupted him, "Of nature. One thing you still have is that gutter mind of yours."

"Nice to know something of who I was is still there," Alec tapped on his head. She smiled, "You seem different than before."

"Amnesia can do that to a person apparently. So what was it like being born with the knowledge to kick ass and take names already?" Alec asked trying to keep the conversation going. "I had a fake life right from the start, so I didn't think much about my memories, just situations that teach us how to deal with them in the future. It's kind of like you being able to know to take cover when someone is shooting at you."

"Never thought of it like that. Back on the Pandora, why did you cuddle up with me on the turn?" he asked. Jane blushed looking away, "Well, I didn't want to be alone and you were the only person still awake. Never liked space battles, only time when I feel helpless."

"Don't feel bad. I feel the same way about space battles. Glad we're able to help each along." He leaned in closer to her. She didn't shy away. She reached forward about to touch Alec's hand when she asked, "So what was up with you and Mira?"

He sighed, leaned back and rolled his eyes, "Why bring that up? There's nothing between us really. Besides, she's way too rough. She stuck something into my eye."

"What?" She sat up straight. Alec explained, "Same thing that Yosemite stuck into my eye. Don't know what it is."

"That sounds strange…so does what's on our sensors." Jane looked over at the monitor seeing an enemy transport flying by. The Alliance's Raven transports looked like cylinders with wings attached to the top. Alec saw the Alliance Eagle fighters looking similar yet smaller and more nimble. Two of them and a Raven flew right in front of them. They were illuminated in red by the display. "Let's see where they go."

Jane moved the Crain right behind them. She kept up with the maneuvers they made in between each of the massive asteroids that drifted in space next to each other.

They varied in size and color from white to gray to brown. Some were made of ice and others of rock. The smaller rocks and dust got deflected off of the energy shields as they passed through the clouds of debris. Alec asked while buckling in to the co-pilots seat, "Weren't we not supposed to see anything for a while?"

"Things change. Besides this is a recon, so someone had to get the right information," Jane explained while maneuvering the Crain in between the asteroids that crashed into each other. Yeager came into the cabin, "So much for sleep."

Jane replied as she did a barrel roll, "We could knock you out again if you need rest."

"And I could cover your eyes to make you a better pilot. At least I didn't need a cuddle buddy to sleep!" He took a set. "Oh shut up, bastard!" Alec fired at him. Yeager looked back with rage in his eye, "What did you say?"

"Not now! Alec, I need you to be gunner while I fly in case things get hot. Yeager, repair anything if it gets broken," Jane ordered as she slowed the Crain down, keeping her distance from the three Alliance crafts. They came upon an asteroid that looked like two Alliance destroyers and a massive cubed shaped mining ship that devoured asteroids as they entered a circular entrance with cutting lasers. There were several other fighter patrols moving around the area as well. Jane set the Crain onto a nearby asteroid, hiding it from the enemy. She started looking around the area, "Stumbled upon a damned hornet's nest. Yeager, send out a drone to get the cavalry."

Yeager tapped on the holo-controls and a round drone was ejected from the Crain and flew off back where they came from. Alec asked, "Now what?"

"Now we play a game of don't get killed. The goal is self-explanatory. The Alliance will more than likely freak out if they see us, so let's just stay put and…" A fighter came right in front of them and stopped. The three of them froze in their seats and looked at the image of it as it turned on search lights. Jane backed off the asteroid and slowly moved the Crain backwards. The light seemed to follow the transport as she hid behind a rock. An outline of the Eagle stayed. When the viewer showed only the smooth stone surface, Yeager yelled, "Stop!"

Jane did so as an image of another fighter suddenly came into view right behind them. Quickly Jane shitted the Crain down and away from the fighter. Alec couldn't help but comment, "The stealth system on this ship is incredible."

Jane laughed, "Yeah, they would have had to have their doors open in order to see us." Suddenly right in front of them was a Raven with its doors open and two people outside doing a spacewalk. One of them was looking right at the Crain. Jane snapped in frustration, "Oh come on! Really?"

The two fighters suddenly came into view and opened fire. The transport was rocked by the hits. Jane moved the Crain down behind the Raven, using it as a shield from the fighters and went backwards trying to get away from them. "I know this might be a little late to ask, but what is this thing armed with?" Alec asked.

"Two sets of laser cutters, fifty missiles, and three sets plasma guns. Would you please fire back?!" She snapped as she flew the Crain backwards under a rock as the two fighters followed were joined by two more. All four of them fired away at the Crain as Jane moved side to side trying to dodge each set of plasma rounds. Alec saw an aiming sight pop up in front of him as the weapons came online. He fired potshots at the fighters with the plasma round hoping to throw them off. He couldn't get a clear shot with the flying rocks and Jane's maneuvers. Alec switched over to missiles and waited for a target lock. The fighters moved too quickly for him to get a good aim. He switched them to proximity mode and fired. A dozen missiles flew out heading towards the Eagles. A couple ran into small rocks and a couple more were shot down. One lucky one got close enough to detonate right next to one of the fighters. The blast sent it flying into an asteroid, bouncing off of that and flying headlong into another Eagle finally shattering into a fiery wreck. "Got one!"

"Took you long enough," Yeager told Alec as he held on. The Crain went vertical, going straight up the side of a rock with the two following fighters peppering the transport with plasma rounds. Alec aimed the laser cannon at the asteroid itself and fired, slicing whole chunks out of it. The fragments popped out in front of the path of the fighters as they moved around trying to dodge the rocks. One of them took a hit leaving it vulnerable. Alec fired again hitting it square in the nose. It was vaporized in the round explosion that followed. He cheered when suddenly they took a hit from a rocket. Jane's console exploded, blinding her. The Crain went flying backwards into the asteroid and bounced off. Several alarms went off inside the cabin as they spun around. Alec looked at the controls, and they seemed familiar to him. "Yeager! Take the guns. I'll fly!"

"What? Do you even know how?" Yeager questioned as Alec moved Jane out of her seat into another and took the controls steering the Crain away from a flying rock. "Yes! Would you man the damned guns already?"

"Weapons control is fried! I have an idea. I'll be back! Don't crash!" He told me going into the cargo compartment. Alec was flying by the seat of his pants, allowing Yeager to act on his instincts. Alec was able to dodge another set of massive rocks. He saw flashes of ships suddenly appear. A different battle flashed in front of his eyes for a second, one with a massive number of Spartan and Alliance ships fighting. Alec blinked several times shaking what he saw and focusing back on the task at hand. He took the joy stick and started operating the controls. Yeager reappeared and told him, "Let them get closer!"

Reluctantly, Alec pulled back just enough to where one of the Alliance fighters was right behind them. Yeager opened one of the cargo hatches and fired a plasma rocket. It flew out and slammed into the Eagle fighter. Its shields popped like a balloon bursting. The next plasma rocket went into the fighter. The force of the explosion caused it to crash and burn, turning a hit rock into a burning comet. "Good job Yeager. One left."

The last Eagle suddenly appeared in front of them about to fire. Alec pushed the engines to full speed, ramming the fighter. It got stuck on the nose of the ship as Alec steered blind. He pushed the boosters to their limits to stop the momentum, and the fighter dislodged and flew off. It crashed right into a floating asteroid. The blast caused enough debris to fly back at the Crain that it caused the craft to lose control. Lights flashed as the ship lost power and went adrift. Alec reached over to Jane, putting her helmet on along with his own and went to the back cargo hold of the dying transport. Yeager stood by the door entrance looking back and said sarcastically, "Great! Next time why don't you just fly into one of the rocks instead of letting us choke to death!"

"Shut up! We're still alive, and we can still be found! Now jump!" Alec pushed him out the door and leaped out with Jane next to him as the Crain flew off. It didn't take long for them to land on a nearby rock. Both Yeager and Alec held onto Jane while punching into the rock to keep themselves from flying off. They held still as the Crain blew up from the inside out. The ball of fire didn't last long as it faded, leaving a dust cloud in its place. "How long will this suits last when it comes to air?" Alec asked.

"It'll last. We just need to go into hibernation. Our suits have beacons installed in case anything like this happens. They won't leave us behind," Yeager told Alec in an oddly reassuring way. "Is it because a mother would never leave her son behind?" Alec asked.

He looked over, "Leave no one behind. Also yes, she wouldn't abandon us. Me especially. Now if you want to save air, try not to talk so much."

Alec nodded and tightened up his grip on Jane. He

took a look at the stars. They never seemed to look so bright even in the belt. He closed his eyes and relaxed. Breathing as they laid there on the rock, he wonder what would come next.

Chapter 9
Decent
2209
Orbit of Mars
A.I.S Caesar
Airlock

"Double check to make sure your gear is good," Lauren ordered as everyone checked each other's armored suits. On each suit was the logo of the company that made them, Iron Clad and the type number, MK II. They covered the whole body with gray metal that was strong enough to take a direct hit with an energy weapon, light enough to move around with ease, enough energy shielding to protect the whole body, and a face mask resembling a human skull for intimidation purposes. There were also multiple places on the suit to put ammo and extra weapons. They were also air tight and had air scrubbers installed so it wouldn't run out of air for some time. Nick asked, "We're not doing the same thing we did last time?"

"Were you sleeping during the briefing again?"

Mindy asked while checking her ammo pouches. Jane told him, "The fucking ship that was supposed to be too damaged to do us any harm managed to not only elude our patrols, but beat us to the station we're heading to. Isn't there a saying about hubris leading to a down fall?"

Lauren snapped, "There's another one. Don't shoot the messenger! I was just conveying information! Don't blame me for that ship managing to survive. Besides, the other side is being more arrogant than we are. If you were at the briefing you would know what I mean!" She looked over at Alec and Tara. He smiled, "No regrets. I have to ask. Why are we still trying to dock with this station if they know we're coming?"

Bryan told him as he moved his joints around making sure his suit wasn't too loose, "The Alliance thinks they can retake this ship from us, so they are letting us dock. Then they are going to try to storm us."

"The ambushers become the ambushed, if you will," Alisa explained while loading up a rocket launcher. Fred nervously asked, "No more non-lethal?"

"One thing about war is it turns bitter and nasty quickly. Might as well roll with it," Duncan donned a juggernaut suit over the already well armored one he had on. This added extra armor and fire power but also made him slow as a turtle. Alec was also putting on the extra armor as they were both taking point. Lauren pulled down her face mask, "Don't wuss out now. We all knew the day would come where people would get hurt. The Alliance isn't going down without a fight, and we aren't going to get to the top without climbing over the slain. Just be thankful that we aren't the first wave."

Tara asked as she loaded up a massive plasma feed machine gun, "What do you mean? I thought we were the vanguard."

"We are, just that the first wave is going to be the cannon fodder to open the door for the rest of us." There was silence as the personnel in front of Squad Thirteen looked back offended but at the same time had the overwhelming look of dread on their faces. Alec snapped, "That's fucked up! Why are we sending people off to the slaughter like that?"

"There's only so much that can be done from armored suits, shields, and weapons. There comes a point where the price of lives is outweighed by the price of territory gained. In order to take this station, there has to be those that go in first to pave the way for the rest. Most of them aren't going to make it. We might not even make it. It's a fact all of you should know. We wearing these armored suits, but we are all equally expendable in order to win. Now the only question any of you should be asking is how many of those assholes can we take down with us?"

"All of them," Fred said while loading up his rifle and then pulling down his face mask. Lauren nodded, "Good. Alter armor camo."

The suits went from a gray color to a digital gray and black pattern. The skeleton heads on their helmets changed to silver. A holographic image of Mars and the station came to view in front of them. Most of Mar's Northern hemisphere was covered in water. Land covered the south. Everything around the equator and the land was green with vegetation. White dots indicated a city. There was only one continent that wasn't attached to the mainland, similar to Australia of Earth. This one was right above the mainland and also surrounded by islands. There were two small oceans in the south, both with plenty of vegetation around them. An ice cap was surrounded by a small forest, and there was a desert in the south. It's a true marvel what could be done with technology. The planet, once a desolate waste land was now a space station.

The station was almost as large as the New Nexus station. It looked like a stack of gray disks stacked on top of each other with a long pull going down to the planet below. There were hundreds of small lights on the surface with slight signs of movement as the station rotated. It got larger the closer the team got. In between each disk was an area for ships to dock in. It looked like a giant cage with tubes inside.

As the ship got into the docking port, several Spartan ships started swarming the area catching the Alliance ships off guard. In the first wave, ten Alliance ships were taken out in hail storm of laser and plasma fire. The last thing they saw were the rest of the ships battling it out and the docking clamps attached to each of the ship's airlocks. It made a sound in the cramped passageway of rubber moving against metal. Energy shields came up in between each squad group. The leading squad wore juggernaut suits with heavy weapons attached, one rocket launcher on each shoulder and two machine guns with plasma ammo on the arms. Alec and Duncan had a similar set up, but only one weapon per arm, one grenade launcher and one machine gun. Squad Thirteen would be the second wave in. No words were spoken as the passageway grew quiet. Everyone kept their stance expecting the inevitable punch that was coming. Alec could hear himself breathing slowly as the monitor showed what was on the other side. Several auto turrets, men with rocket launchers, and machine gunners lay out on the deck. Alec sighed, "This is going to suck."

"Suck our genitals more like it," Duncan nudged him. Alec laughed, "Why not?"

The doors opened suddenly with both sides briefly staring at each other with weapons at the ready. The Alliance soldiers only had on basic battle gear: helmets, armored vests, knee pads and elbow pads. But they were armed with energy weapons. Their eyes were visible enough to see the whites as they went wide seeing the juggernauts. The very next second both sides open fired on each other. The juggernauts were temporarily protected by the one-way energy shield that lit up when it was being hit. They fired back, focusing all their fire on the turrets. It took a couple of plasma rockets, but they went down hard sending shards of metal into the air. The energy shield went down in a bright flash and the two juggernauts started getting hit with energy rounds.

As they fired blindly, the two behind them pushed them forward and everyone moved up towards the exit. The first two juggernauts fell and the second two took their place pressing forward with the rest of the first wave charging out the door forming a perimeter. Alec and Duncan went forward right up to the airlock door itself witnessing the destruction. The two juggernauts were Jane and Lauren lookalikes. Their suits were filled with burnt holes and smoke rising from each one. They managed to take out at least three dozen Alliance soldiers. Most of them were blown in half with each half almost completely burnt. Some were taken out by shrapnel and a few unlucky ones were still alive despite their wounds. They could see in other parts of the station where other teams were pushing the Alliance back. The enemy soldiers began to break ranks running to the passageways that they still held.

Lauren came up behind the team, tapping their shoulders to indicate it was time to move out. Both Duncan and Alec crouched down bracing themselves to move forward. The other juggernauts managed to clear a path for them to go. The energy field in front of them went down in a flash and the two of them bolted out the ship's airlock. Next to them in other airlocks came streams of Spartan personnel charging out into the next area. Alec and Duncan had to hop over the dead bodies in order not to slip. Alec stepped on one, crushing the person's ribcage as a loud bone popping sound filled the air. He kept his balance and kept moving.

Several flashes of light flew by them as Alec ran to a corner. He let his body slam into the wall as the rest of the squad formed up behind him. On the opposite side, others were getting ready to do the same. After getting tapped on the shoulder again, Alec and Duncan went around the corner facing a wall of enemy soldiers. Without thinking, they both sides fired. Their shields flashed with every hit as they kept moving forward. The grenade rounds launched with such force that they went through the armored vests of the Alliance soldiers. Soon after the grenades detonated, all that was left of said soldiers were the limbs. Alec held down his machine gun trigger cutting through them easily. The rounds left massive burn holes in their bodies before they dropped to the deck. It practically cooked them with the amount of heat in each round. The Alliance soldiers pulled back leaving the floor covered in dead bodies and parts for the Spartans to walk over. Alec paused as a woman lying on the floor grabbed his leg. She was missing her other arm and legs and was gagging on her own blood. Jane stepped on her arm and shot her in the head, "Be polite, and put them out of their misery."

He nodded as he kept going. The Alliance soldiers broke rank completely and were fully running away from the Spartans. Both Duncan and Alec got carried away and chased after them. They were going to round the corner, but both Alisa and Tara grabbed them and yanked them back. The other two juggernauts ran forward and got shot up by the ambushing fire. Enraged, Alec ran across the wide passageway and leaped forward, sliding on his chest plate. He ended up right in front of a line of soldiers that aimed their weapons at him. He had them in his sights first. Alec fired, making their bodies fly apart after every hit. Duncan covered his back taking the other side. Fred and Nick pulled Alec back up and pushed him forward. They used him for cover as they fired back at the fleeing Alliance personnel. Alec saw they were on a catwalk above a massive round metal elevator. It was almost twenty stories tall, had windows spread throughout, and looked like a spin top with a metal rod coming out the top and bottom. Lauren suddenly pushed both Alec and Duncan over the guardrail, causing them to fall down toward the elevator. Duncan asked, "Did she just push us?"

"I think we should worry about the landing!" Alec said as they slammed on top of the elevator. Both of them were able to get back up from the dents they left on the roof. They came under fire from the level above them. Duncan and Alec went back to back and moved in a circle firing back at the enemy. Glass and dead bodies fell down on top of them. They emptied the last of their grenade rounds onto the balconies above. A ring of fire came flying out from the blast sending burnt bodies, glass and shards of metal down on top of the elevator. The others in the team came sliding down on the massive pillar to the elevator roof. Alec was suddenly hit with a rocket round that knocked him down. It got overly hot in his suit and he quickly started stripping off his juggernaut armor and weapons as they were melting from the heat. Once Alec was back down to his basic armored suit, Mindy pushed him into a hole leading inside the elevator itself. He landed on his feet and snapped, "Why is everyone pushing me?"

Jane told him while handing him a plasma rifle, "Everyone needs a push to get going. Come on!"

He followed her down a passageway that was cramped and barley lit. Alec ducked down after Jane fired a couple rounds. He saw a brief shadow that got hit and fell to the deck. She went forward leaving the man in agony as he held his throat. Alec aimed for his head and fired a round, "Mercy's a bullet."

Alec caught up with Jane as she cleared a corner motioning him to follow. He went forward when a rifle stock went into his face. Alec fell flat on his back as he saw a woman aiming a rifle at him. She was suddenly shot in the chest, going down instantly. Duncan, without his juggernauts suit on either, helped him up, "Can't let these bastards get you down."

Alec laughed, "Always get back up!"

The two of them caught up to Jane as she reached to open a door. Fred ran up right behind Alec. The two of them positioned themselves to storm in. Jane opened the door, and Alec threw a frag grenade. They heard yelling just before it went off. Alec went in first clearing the left, with Jane clearing the right. Fred cleared the center. Alec swept his rifle firing at anyone who came in his sights. The enemies dropped like dominos after having holes burned into their chest. "Clear!"

"All clear!" Alec replied. Duncan moved in and went to work on the control console. He placed a hack on the computer and activated the elevator. The room lit up showing the carnage around them. Duncan said, "All systems activated!"

Lauren's voice announced, "Good. Hold there while the rest of us clear out the elevator."

"Roger," Jane said while covering the only exit and entrance to the room. Duncan yelled, "Let's do that again!"

"It's going to be a long war. I'm positive we will do it again!" Alec laughed as Fred replied, "Are you kidding me? People died! There are fucking dead people in this fucking room!"

"Come on. If people didn't die, life wouldn't be as fun," Jane said while kneeling down making herself comfortable while moving one of the dead bodies aside. Fred yelled, "I just don't think killing should be taken so lightly!"

"Now you must be kidding. These suits were fucking heavy! Plus that grenade launcher kicked like a bull. Don't tell us it was light," Alec snapped at him enjoying his relief from the weights. Fred went on, "Crazy bastards! This guy is missing his head!"

"Guess like he's not getting ahead in life! I've always wanted to do a one liner like that!" Duncan laughed as he showed security footage of the elevator being secured. Back up forces started rushing inside the elevator as Lauren said, "Elevator is secure. Once I'm up there, start the descent."

"Roger," Jane said as she relaxed her position. Fred lifted up his mask, "Poor bastards didn't have a chance…"

"Who's the one telling bad jokes now? We lost people, too! Hell, most of the first wave got killed. They had a chance. They'll have them again," Duncan snapped as Alec added, "To suck our genitals!"

Jane laughed, "Damn straight. Not going to suck themselves. Fred, this is a fucked up situation, but you can't let it get to you. They had a chance to hurt us just like we had a chance to hurt them. As it's said, all's fair in love and war."

"Only bad thing that happens in love is an infection! These people got fucking mutilated!" Fred yelled looking guilty and engaged at the same time. Jane went on, "Did you really think it wasn't going to get bloody? You've had years to think about when it would. What did you expect?"

"Guess shooting at holograms doesn't do the real thing justice. Why did you have to turn on the lights? And that smell…" he started throwing up. Duncan laughed, "Iron stomach! Don't see us losing our lunch!"

"Shouldn't have taken off your mask. Don't be worried about mortality. Live in the moment. Don't lose your balls now," Jane told him. Fred breathed, "Metaphorically or literally?"

"Both," Alec patted him on the back. Lauren came in with the others following, "Okay, drop this bitch. We're coming home!"

"Hell yeah!" Duncan tapped away on the controls as the elevator moved. Everyone had the sudden sensation of dropping. Lauren smiled, "Good work everyone! The other teams secured the station and the orbit of Mars! We'll be in the atmosphere soon. I know I've said this before, but it's not going to get any easier. When we go planet side, we're going to be going up against tanks, Mechs, and fighters. Jane and I will fetch us some heavy weapons. Stay put."

Everyone stared as Lauren walked out of the room leaving the rest of the squad in there to ponder. Nick sighed, "Well, looks like we aren't going to be shooting fish in a barrel again."

Tara sat down, "Sounds like fun to me. Small fries get old eventually."

"Well, now that we got time to kill, why did you

join the Sparta Corps?" Alec asked wanting to get to know her better. She told him, "I was bored. I wanted an adrenaline rush. If facing mortality isn't a good way to do it, I can think of at least one other way that is."

"You would have thought we'd talk a little earlier. Why not?" Duncan asked as Alisa bluntly told him, "We're either training, or stuck in cryo tubes. Not very much time for anything else. Amazing we know each other's names."

"I joined because it was that or go back to prison…" Nick said as everyone looked at him oddly. "Oh come on! I know Alec's been in the pen before."

"Jail and a penitentiary are two different thing. So drop the soap much?" Alec asked with a smile. Nick shrugged it off, "We had liquid soap. Kind of hard to drop that."

"He's trying to ask if you were forced into anything," Tara sighed trying to get to the point. Nick answered innocently, "They forced me to take pills and wake up early. Jerks."

"Did you suffer abuse from your fellow inmates?" Duncan asked probing even more. Nick sighed, "They would always make fun of me! They said I couldn't do anything right."

Alisa snapped, "Oh just say it! Did you or did you not get molested?"

Nick looked shocked, "What? No! You think I was the one getting molested? I was always on top! Didn't think I would establish dominance first? I had to. It was the only way to get respect."

"You raped your inmates?" Bryan asked in shock. Nick nodded, "It's about power and humiliation! It was either that or be a drug mule! I did that on the outside. I wasn't going to do it on the inside!"

Bryan held up his hand saying, "Okay! That's enough! We got the hint. Prison sucks. Don't let me catch you next to me when I'm trying to sleep, just saying. So Fred, why did you join?"

"That's a good question. Why did you join if you wuss out when things get bloody?" Mindy asked pushing aside one of the dead bodies to get a seat. Fred sighed, "I wanted to make a difference, change things for once. I got tired of the leadership on Earth and the puppets who're running the show."

"As opposed to the puppets we're about to put into power? Got a real reason besides this bullshit we've been fed?" Alec asked. Fred sighed, "I got tired of being a sheep! I hated my mundane life, mundane job, and my mundane existence! Like Tara, I needed a change. Good enough reason?"

"Only got to justify your actions to who's in the

mirror. As long as you're cool with it, fine," Duncan said to him. Fred laughed, "Yeah. Guess I should lighten up a little more."

"Just don't get overly dominating like some people," Mindy looked over to Nick, "No regrets!"

"No more regrets…" Fred said. The room suddenly rocked and alarms went off. There was a violent, loud crash as smoke filled the room and everything went dark.

CHAPTER 10
SMASH AND GRAB
2214
SOL SYSTEM ASTEROID BELT
CRAIN TRANSPORT
CARGO AREA

ALEC felt a slap on the face as he came to. He saw Kathryn, Cullen, and Mira standing over him. Yeager and Jane were waking up themselves. Alec sighed, "Thanks for coming for us."

"You're not going to be saying that when I tell you what we're doing next," Lauren told him as she pulled up holographic images of the cubed shaped mining ship. "Like Victor said, no rest for the weary. While you were passed out, we've been setting up an ambush in the asteroids. We rigged a couple of them to fly into the escort ships while we fly onto the mining ship itself and grab what we need. Once that's done, we get out. One of our destroyers will be providing cover for us while we go in, and they'll be picking us up. Any questions?"

"What kind of security does the mining ship have?" Jane asked while rubbing her eyes. Mira told her, "To be honest, we're kind of going in blind on this one. As far as we could gather, they mostly have auto turrets. We suspect there might be a platoon of Alliance soldiers on board as well along with reinforcements on the two escort ships."

"All the more reason to get this done quickly," Cullen commented. Yeager asked, "If faster than light travel is illegal, why is the Alliance gathering partials to do it?"

Kathryn explained, "It can also be used to make a star go supernova."

Alec got up when he heard this. Holding his head he said, "So you're telling me that a form of space travel is outlawed while weapons that can wipe out a whole solar system are acceptable?" He paused to think about the whole situation, "These aliens sure have their priorities backwards, don't they?"

Kathryn sighed while looking down, "I'm just saying what Yosemite told us. Would it also be a surprise to know that the weapons came first... leading to said travel limitations?"

"Destruction is more important than travel? Really?" Alec laughed to himself.

"In their defense, both the Vegans and the

Stallions run this galaxy," Kathryn told him. He asked, "Guess blowing shit up is a good way to get to the top. So how would said travel device work?"

Mira showed him a holographic image, "It affects space time by causing any object inside a bubble or warp field to stay still in one point of space time while the whole universe moves. So time and space would move, but not a ship inside the bubble. Got to love loopholes about not being able to go faster than light."

"Kind of like the wormholes?" Alec asked feeling like he'd heard this before. Cullen went on, "In a manner of speaking. Only thing with wormholes, everything is connected in real time. Even if we see light that has been traveling centuries or eons from its source, we could still be in the same time zone with the star systems that the light originated from. So you could talk to someone across the galaxy like we're talking right now across a room with no time lag. That's how the Vegans and Stallions are able to have interstellar empires."

Jane even jumped in on the discussion, "The thing about warp travel is that time stands still for the object inside while everything else moves on. It can be unpredictable if misused. It could possibly be used as a form of time travel, mostly for going forward in time fast, but there are theories about going back instead. That's another reason it's been outlawed."

"Never knew you all were so well versed in physics," Alec said in genuine surprise. Yeager condescendingly told him, "Kind of have to be in order to last in space. Oh yeah, nice flying."

"Like you could have done better!" Alec got defensive about it. He went on, "I was paying you a compliment for once, but if you want to be an ass about it, fine."

"How was I to know you were being nice? If you want to give me a compliment, don't start off by busting my balls over physics!"

"Can you both please stop? Can we get back to infiltrating the giant asteroid eating cube now? We'll have plenty of time to bicker when this is over!" Kathryn snapped. Alec didn't give up, "Really? I never seem to have the time! I've been overly occupied with flying across this system to kill people I've never heard of. Not to mention, I still can't remember much about my past. I don't even know if the people in my memories are still alive. I barely know anything about you. Jane, you're a clone who can fly. Kathryn, you're an android that got knocked up somehow. Cullen, you're the son of a man that I used to know. Mira, you're kind of a sadist. And Yeager, you're some five year old cybernetic freak who hates my guts! That's it! Who are you people?"

"We're the ones with a plan. Either stay on and find out what you want to know, or wimp out. Seeing how you've been rolling with things so far, I don't think you're going to back out now. So if you would kindly calm down and let Kathryn finish the brief?" Yeager told him bluntly. Stunned, Alec sat down, "Fine. Sorry to interrupt."

"Thanks, Yeager. Like I said, this is a smash and grab. We go in through the airlock, use a scanner to lead us to the partials, get the some of the partials and get out. Now get ready. The fireworks are about to start," she told them while showing an image of the nearby area. They were holding still in the area where the last Crain was destroyed. The asteroids around them started moving on their own. Each one was rigged with engines and propelled themselves into the enemy vessels before they could react. The first ship got hit on its side. The hull crumpled in with its metal plates folding up together like an accordion. Small shards of rocks flew off from the impact. Several flashes came from the breaches inside the vessel. The other ship got hit from above, dead center, right where all the essential areas were. When the asteroid pushed halfway into the destroyer, she exploded from the inside out breaking up into pieces like a plate hitting a floor. The massive mining ship took the most abuse with seven asteroids sent flying at the vessel. All of them hit in the vulnerable flat sides of the ship, yet the giant rocks only left dents in its hull.

The last Spartan frigate came into view with a fighter wing. The Crain they were in started to follow along. Their escorts opened fire on the surviving destroyer. The triangular ship blasted away at the weakened section of the ship with its torpedoes, easily bashing though the breaches. It didn't take long before the ship went down in a ball of fire. Everything that didn't burn was thrown into space to drift. The transport the team was on went ahead into the debris field, swerving to avoid the objects left over from the collision. Alec pulled his helmet back down as the Crain closed in. He got handed a plasma rifle as the others checked their armaments. "Remember, quick in, quick out. Use your jet packs effectively. We only have twenty minutes before Alliance reinforcements arrive. Once we have a partial sample, do not let anything happen to it! It makes nuclear warheads look like fireworks," Kathryn reminded them.

"Wait. If the partial is really that dangerous, then why are we throwing giant rocks at the ship carrying it?" Alec asked. She looked over at him, "It's a risk we have to take in order to get the damned thing. Besides, who said anything about this being safe?"

"Sorry I asked," Alec mumbled not even really thinking about it. It reminded him of the expendable speech her sister gave. When they got close to the mining ship, they came upon a breach in the hull they would use for their insertion. The transport hovered right over the opening as the doors opened up. Cullen went first leaping across the void and into the ship. He signaled for the rest of the team to follow. Mira went next pulling a metal containment box with her. Alec followed once she was in. He relied on inertia to get him to the other side. Cullen grabbed Alec's free arm and pulled him inside.

This ship was different from the others. It had a wide square hull that didn't have the airlocks at every interval. The lights flickered on and off sporadically. Alec switched his optics so it wouldn't mess with his vision. Once everyone was on board they went forward into the ship. The gravity was down so they used boosters that were added onto the armored suits. It felt like swimming as they moved through the ship. Cullen and Alec were in front so they checked the corners when they came up. Alec checked around one of them and saw a person. He almost fired when he took a closer look and saw the person was already dead. There were three people floating around the adjacent passageway with their hands on their own throats and the look of suffocation on their cold bodies. They didn't look military, nor did they have on protective suits. Alec wondered how many others got caught in the crossfire.

He moved on as they got to a door that was labeled Hazardous Storage. Alec went to one side of the door while the rest of the team lined up on the other. He reached over and placed a charge on the groove in between two part door. It made a quiet flash as the door split apart. He grabbed one side, and Kathryn grabbed the other. Both of used their boosters to pry it open. Jane and Yeager went in first. "Clear!" they proclaimed in unison.

"All clear!" was said over the radio. Alec went around into the door and saw a massive storage unit in the middle of the room. There were several warning signs alerting them to the danger of what was inside. Mira slowly opened up the storage unit's door and a bright light flashed almost blinding the team. It didn't take long before the partial sample was collected. "Got it!" exclaimed Mira.

"All right. Let's get out of here." Kathryn said. They got out of the storage room quickly and backtracked down the same hallway they came from. The team rounded a corner. There were Alliance soldiers coming from the opposite direction. Both groups were surprised to see each other and froze for a second. It didn't take long before everyone drew down on one another. Alec and his friends fired first using their boosters to counteract the recoil of their rifles. The Alliance soldiers now had energy shielding, and it flashed when hit. Kathryn rocketed forward while dodging weapon fire. She went right in front of an Alliance soldier, shot the rifle out of the person's hand and punched the soldier in the face mask. The hit was hard enough to dent the metal. Blood and air came out of the cracks. She used the soldier as a shield while the other Alliance members tried to fire at her.

Alec and the others took advantage and charged forward. His boosters blasted along with his rifle as he went forward. The soldier he was hitting flew backwards like a rag doll bouncing around the bulkheads. All of them broke though the Alliance line and bolted down the passageway headed for the exit. The Alliance was right behind firing potshots. The team threw grenades to slow the Alliance down as the shockwaves from the explosions seemed to speed the team up. The breach came up and they each went for the transport. The box with the partial inside was the first thing to go. Alec was the last one to leap out into space as the Crain started moving away from the mining ship. The ship was almost out of reach. Alec didn't know if he could make the jump. Suddenly, Jane reached out grabbing his hand so he wouldn't be left behind. Alec held on tightly as he felt someone grab his leg. There was a soldier holding on for dear life while trying to shoot Alec with a pistol. He started kicking over and over again to get the person off of him. The soldier lost his grip on the pistol and tried using a plasma knife instead. Jane held on to his arm as the transport maneuvered though the asteroid field. When the soldier tried to stab him, Alec kicked the knife out of his hands. The transport came in for a hot landing as the frigate was also making a run for it. Alec's leg felt like it was going to be ripped off as the Crain increased speed in order to make a landing inside.

Alec felt himself get pulled into the transport as the others started to help Jane. They entered the hanger bay of the frigate and came to a sudden stop. Alec went flying into the Crain with the soldier right with him. The two of them slammed into the bulkhead and bounced off. Alec took the opportunity to grab the soldier and throw a punch right into the face mask. The hit was so hard it ripped the mask off of the soldier's face. Her thin eyes went wide as she started gasping for air. The woman looked familiar to him, but he didn't know why. She reached around as she started choking, trying to breathe in oxygen that wasn't there. It didn't take long before she suffocated going still in the vacuum. Yeager grabbed the dead body and threw her into the transport hard enough that her head slammed into the bulkhead and she stopped moving. Mira and

Cullen grabbed the box and headed out of the transport. Everyone else followed as the mechanics started repairs on the Crain. Alec drifted out of the transport seeing the damage of mining ship being bashed against the asteroids. Each impact caused more damage as the dents turned to full on tears. White clouds of leaking air came out as flashes of light came from the hull breaches. From behind her, five other Alliance ships appeared. The outer doors to the hanger bay closed as a voice came over the intercom, "All hands, conducting warp testing. Brace for shock."

Alec went to the nearest bulkhead and pulled up an image of what was going on outside. There was a quick flash of light from the mining ship as the cargo must have gone critical. In that brief second, he saw a shock wave rip from the center of the vessel, impacting the Alliance ships. They vanished in an instant, flattened on impact. The asteroids around the area turned to dust and a massive cloud came at the ship. It rocked as the prototype drive onboard was activated. Alec's head suddenly went against the bulkhead.

CHAPTER 11
2209
BEACH HEAD
MARS
BIBIDIS PETEERA

ALEC was suddenly pulled up and got a slap upside his helmet. He heard, "Wake up!"

Lauren was about to slap him again when he caught her hand, "I'm awake! Never knew you were programmed for bondage."

She slapped his arm away, "Not now!"

He switched his optics over to night vision and saw the ceiling in the room they were in had collapsed. Tara and Nick were pulling Mindy from the rubble. Jane and Duncan were crawling out from the debris. Alisa attended to Bryan who was crying in pain as he tried to reattach his shin to his leg. The wound was cauterized, so there wasn't any chance of him bleeding out. His armor plating and clothing were pulled out of the way on the whole leg, giving easier access to the wound. Alisa used medical gel from her med kit, put it on both ends of wound and placed the shin back on the leg. She motioned for Nick to hold the limb in place. Alisa warned him, "This is going to hurt."

"Really? How could it hurt any more than the pain I'm already in?" Bryan wept as she pulled a medical stapler right above the gap. "How about this?" she asked.

He suddenly cried harder as the organic staples went into his leg. The staples dissolved, regenerating parts of his skin, reattaching the bone and reconnecting the nerves. The new skin looked like it had been water logged. Nick used gauze and metal shards to immobilize Bryan's leg. Mindy asked, "Hey, where's Fred?"

Lauren went over to the rubble and started moving it around franticly. Alec tried getting up almost bumping his head on a beam. There were small fires in the room making it hard to see, not to mention sparks flying around above. The metal shards clattered as Lauren threw them aside. She suddenly stopped and muttered, "Fred's dead."

"Oh come on! Just because Fred rhymes with dead doesn't mean anything!" Mindy said in denial. Lauren replied, "He's dead. Trust me on this one!"

"Come on. He was wearing an armored suit! How could he…" She went up to Lauren and saw what she saw. Lauren snapped with some sadness in her voice, "His torso, as you can see, has been crushed! He's dead! Still don't trust me? I dare you to open his helmet and find out!"

"Fred is dead!" Mindy said in shock stepping back. Lauren slapped her across her face mask, "Get a grip! We still have a job to do. We'll mourn later. Got it?"

"Fine." Mindy walked off slowly as Lauren went back and pulled Alec forward and out into the hallway. It was surprisingly in good shape. Jane handed anti-vehicle rocket launchers to everyone. Lauren told them, "Split up the ammo that would have gone to Fred, Bryan and Tara."

"Wait. Why aren't I getting any rockets?" Bryan asked still in tears." She looked down at him, "That gel is only meant to keep your limb intact. If you move around, it'll fall off. I also need someone to stay here with you and make sure you get proper medical follow up. Want a phony limb?"

"No..." He sighed accepting his immobility. Lauren went on, "Tara, I don't want to lose anyone else today. Watch him."

She nodded tapping Bryan on the shoulder. She grabbed a sniper rifle and motioned for everyone to follow, "Everyone else follow me."

They formed a single file to go down the hallway. It looked like it had been hit over and over from the outside with the way the walls and ceiling bulged inward. There were sparks and smoke filling the passage as they went towards an exit. They crouched down, making sure they didn't sweep each other with their rifle muzzles. It didn't take long before they came upon an opening. It was a breach in the elevator that allowed them to look outside. Lauren looked out and shared what she saw to the others in a camera feed. The elevator look like it had taken a hit and fell most of the way down. It was sitting on top of a dented door blocking it from the landing platform. There was a constant groan of metal as the door bent slightly under the pressure. Surprisingly, the support column was still intact. The landing platform looked like an upside down pyramid meant to catch the cone shaped elevator. The shiny reflective exterior looked crumpled from the force of the impact and also moaned from the pressure. The landing platform was dwarfed by the four mountains nearby: Parsonis, Arsal, Aseraeus and the massive Olympus.

The blue sky showed the hundreds of clouds of smoke rising into the air. Several thousand transports fell from the sky. The freights came down for close support. Each of them burned on entry looking like a meteor shower. There were even more fighters all flying up in the air to engage each other. The Alliance had weapons platforms that could shoot at objects in space. They looked like a gray, single lens telescope. It could turn around in any direction and fire out a massive partial beam. One such blast took down a freight. The explosion was large enough that the elevator even rocked. The large elevator looked like it had taken some hits and fell from above. At the elevator, other Spartan operatives survived the drop. They leapt out from the elevator exposed on the roof top. From below came three Alliance Eagle fighters hovering up. Lauren came on the communications, "Enemy fighters! Hit the deck!"

It was too late. They opened fire. A wave of plasma rounds hit the operatives below. Their shields quickly went down and their armor got so hot it melted into the occupants of the suits, killing them instantly. The dead were frozen in place as the metal cooled down. Lauren quickly fired off a plasma rocket that spiraled as it propelled forward into one of the fighters. The blast sent it down as well as taking out its shielding. Nick quickly followed with another rocket. The wounded fighter deployed decoys and a massive amount of flares appeared around the craft. The rocket missed. Lauren got off one more shot, landing it right on top of the cockpit. The impact caused the Eagle to seem to float temporarily before it went up in a bigger blast. The other two fighters quickly opened fire on the team's location. Lauren pushed back against the others as they had to go backwards in a squatting position. The metal around the team got red hot as the round impacted over and over. After a rocket impacted into the elevator part of the floor gave away suddenly sending Lauren, Nick, Alec and Alisa tumbling down. They fell out of the elevator and down onto the roof top. They each landed on their feet as the roof started to give way under the weight. One of the fighters broke off from shooting the elevator and fired another rocket down at the roof. They leaped out of the way as the metal roof bounced like a drum being hit. The impact was enough to start a chain reaction causing it to collapse. The elevator slid into the platform as the roof caved in. Lauren snapped, "Run!"

The four of them sprinted as fast as they could across the collapsing metal doors as they bent inward towards the complex. It didn't help matters that the Eagle was still firing at them. They had to make long leaps in order to dodge the fire. The sound of impacting rounds and bending metal screeched though the air. Alec leaped up, spun around and fired a rocket at the fighter. The rocket sent the craft backwards giving the others enough time to fire their own rounds. One fighter took two direct hits flying off to its flaming crash sight. The other took a hit, too, making it lose its shielding. Alec suddenly found himself falling into the complex right along with the sliding metal plates. Nick leaped down grabbing Alec's legs and held on for dear life. Soon his grip was lost and both of them started to plummet. Lauren leaped down and grabbed them both. She started pulling them up when the Eagle came right down, close enough to where they could feel the pressure from the engines beating down upon them. Before it could fire, Alisa shot off a rocket just in time to hit the fighter square in the nose. It went flying backward aimlessly firing rounds as it disappeared behind the edge of the complex. It was soon followed by a tower of fire and black smoke. The elevator came to a crashing halt as it claimed into its landing platform down below. Lauren pulled them up asking, "You guys all right?"

Alec nodded as Nick said, "I guess, seeing how we didn't die from literally falling from the sky. Alliance can't shoot for shit!"

They suddenly heard a loud scream. Alisa pulled off her face mask. It was steaming with heat as she cried. Her face was burned with blisters all over it. Her eyes fell out of her head as she leaned down screaming. Lauren ran over and quickly injected her with some pain killers. Alisa gasped as both Nick and Alec screamed, "Shit!"

"Give me some fucking medical gel!" Lauren snapped at them. Nick pulled out a small spray bottle and handed it off. Lauren started dousing the wounds with the gel as it stopped the bleeding and swelling. Alec knelt down grabbing her hand, "Don't worry! You'll be fine! They can fix this!"

Alisa rasped loudly, "Not soon enough assholes!"

Lauren gave her another dose of the pain medicine and she helped Alisa up, "What's going on?"

"We're going to have to find a way down to the rest of the team. Also we can't leave you here," Lauren told her. Alisa countered, "I have no damned eyes! I'm fucking combat ineffective!"

"You're not fighting, just walking. Any other team members, roger up," Lauren called over the radio. No one answered. "We need to find a way down that doesn't involve falling."

"Want to take the stairs?" Nick asked sarcastically. Lauren screamed, "Incoming!"

From above came a Falcon transport firing off a missile at them. The hit caused the metal they were standing on to slide down on top of the elevator. Lauren motioned for the others to follow her. Alec grabbed Alisa's hand and pulled her along as they ran forward along the sliding metal slab as it bent downward. The dust and debris hid their movement long enough for them to make a jump. They leaped towards the pillar and grabbed on. All of them slid down to the elevator's roof as the metal shard went falling behind them with a loud clank echoing in the destroyer landing pad. Lauren ordered, "Hide!"

They ducked down underneath the wreckage as the Falcon came down lower in a hover. The side doors opened up as Alliance soldiers inside got ready to leap out. "Wait for them to get lower before we attack," Lauren commanded.

Suddenly plasma rounds started flying at the transport with operatives falling dead, missing body parts plummeting. From a pile of rubble, Duncan and Tara rose up firing away with their rifles. Mindy and Jane ran towards the transport as it turned to face its attackers. They both leaped up into the Falcon as several more soldiers came flying out like flies. The transport suddenly went crashing down right on top of the already dead operatives. Alec asked, "Still want us to wait?"

"Come on!" She and the others charged ahead. They climbed into the Flacon seeing several dead soldiers still strapped in on the deck. The air stunk with the scent of burning metal and bodies. They made their way to the cockpit where both Jane and Mindy were struggling with the pilots. They were both putting up a fight for being shorter than the two operatives in armor. They held their weapons at bay while dodging their punches. Two shots rang out and the two pilots dropped dead missing part of their heads. Everyone looked back at Alisa who was holding a plasma pistol, "Guess I'm not that ineffective after all."

Tara and Duncan hopped onboard the transport. Lauren asked, "Where's Bryan? I told you to stay with him."

"He is with us... mostly," Tara explained turning around. Both of Bryan's legs were gone, and he was on Tara's back like a pack. "Stay behind you said, wait around you said. Really good idea!" yelled Bryan.

"Get off my ass! You were crippled and couldn't walk!" Lauren snapped. Bryan yelled, "She looks like her face got fried and you brought her! Double standards much?"

"At least I can still walk!" Alisa spoke as loud as she could. Bryan scoffed, "I can still see. I can make out how ugly your burned ass face is!"

"I can't do this!" Alisa went forward and kicked him in the groin making him cry. Tara turned around, "Hey! Mind what's behind your target!"

"Worth it!" She laughed, Lauren slammed her fist into the bulkhead, "Enough! We didn't go through a shit load of training to turn into brats when shit hits the fan! Now we're taking this flying bastard to the damned orbital platforms. We'll wing it from there! Jane, get her up in the air."

Jane hopped in the pilot's seat and tapped the holographic controls. The Falcon went back up in the air and out of the complex. So far, only a few ground forces had landed. They were pinned down by the armored hover tanks that looked like metal boxes with cannons sticking out of them. The enemy fighters seemed to be holding their air space while the enemy Mechs were knocking transports out of the sky like it was target practice. Their massive handheld weapons, which looked like giant sniper rifles, fired a partial round that packed a mean punch. Two shots and a Crain would go down in flames. The heavy ships couldn't get in close enough to provide effective orbital support because of the massive weapons platforms. That's where they were heading. The transport they were in blended in with the rest of the Alliance defenders. That also meant they were targeted by their own. Jane suddenly maneuvered the craft as one of their own Eagle fighters fired at them. Alec asked, "Why do they call it friendly fire when it seems overly hostile?"

Lauren hopped into the co-pilot's seat and activated the weapons. Mindy asked, "Wait, you aren't going to fire back are you?"

"I'll show them what friendly fire is!" Lauren fired

back at the fighters around them. The partial blast sent them back as their shields flashed from the hits. One fighter was left exposed enough that it was taken out with a missile. A fragment impacted the transport knocking everyone around. Alarms went off indicating the damage was severe. They were almost to one of the platforms. Lauren went on the radio and called out, "Mayday, mayday. We're going down hot!" She cut of the radio, "Fly us into one of the damned platforms!"

"Did you really have to get our own people killed?" Tara asked as she strapped herself into a chair along with everyone else. Lauren snapped, "I want to fucking win! Deal with the damned grief afterwards! Shut up and brace for shock!"

The transport dove down onto the platform. Jane aimed for one of the legs as they got lower. She did her best to level their angle of approach. The Falcon bounced up against the rock before going nose first into the ground. The transport started flipping over itself going forward. It came to a sudden stop after a dozen rolls on the ground. The transport looked like a beat up can with dents all over. Inside there were sparks and flashing light adding to the confusion. Lauren pushed her way out of the smashed cockpit with her helmet ripped off along with part of her face showing her cold artificial skull. She reached back and pulled her arm from the twisted metal and reattached it to her body. Alec dropped from his seat and slowly got up trying to maintain his balance, "Where's Jane?"

"She's dead. Let's move on to those still alive. Who else is up?" There was a moment of quiet with only the ambient sound of weapons fire echoing in the background. She asked again, "Who's up?"

"I am," Tara, Duncan, Nick and Mindy said as they got out of their seats. Bryan cried, "I can't get up!"

"You never could get it up, limp dick!" Alisa snapped as she felt her way around the environment, still blinded. Bryan snapped as he burst into tears, "I'm fucking paralyzed you asshole! I can't move!"

Alec went over and saw a metal spike sticking out of Bryan's back as he trembled in pain. "I think my suit's defective," complained Bryan.

Lauren pushed her way up to him, "You and Alisa stay behind. You look, and she'll shoot..."

"Leaving people behind really worked out the last time for me, didn't it?" Bryan yelled at her. She told him bluntly, "You're still alive. It worked. Everyone else, let move out!"

She motioned from them to follow. Alisa grabbed a rifle and sat next to Bryan waiting for the enemy to come. They stacked up next to a door as Alliance soldiers gathered around outside. Lauren opened the door and lunged forward, impaling a soldier's head with her fingers. She used the body as a shield as she opened fire. The others quickly followed charging outside and firing away. This caught the attention of a hundred others nearby. Lauren shouted, "Go for the damned platform!"

She fired grenade rounds at the oncoming soldiers to hold them off. All of them got down to the prone position and crawled towards them taking pot shots. Everyone was almost blinded from the light of weapons firing in the sky. These weapons were more powerful than the ones they dealt with before. The team took cover behind the large leg of the platform as hits landed around them. As they leaned against the metal wall, Duncan asked, "How are we going to get up there?"

Lauren pulled the burnt, severed head from her hand and then pulled out two long knives, "Use the heat to dig into the metal, then turn down the power when you put your weight on the handle. Watch me!"

She leaped up onto the leg and stabbed into the metal with the two hot knives melting the metal. As she hung up there she ordered, "Alec and Duncan, on me. Tara, Nick, and Mindy, cover us!"

Mindy, Nick and Tara laid down on the dirt taking turns firing at the oncoming Alliance soldiers as they closed in. Duncan and Alec started their climb up the platform. They went as fast as they could with partial rounds landing around them. As they neared the top, Duncan took a hit causing him to lose his grip on the knives. Alec reached down grabbing him just in time. His arms were stretched holding on to the lodged knife and Duncan's hand at the same time. Lauren flipped over, hanging from her feet upside down and fired back at the soldiers. Alec swung Duncan up to a catwalk. Duncan grabbed on and swung Alec up as well. Both of them went over the top and onto the metal frame. The two of them quickly got up and ran towards the control booth hanging underneath the platform. Both of them got on either side of the door with their weapons prepped at a high ready. Duncan placed a charge on the door blowing it open. Alec went in first, sweeping the room from the center to the left corner. The personnel inside went for their side arms. Alec shot them before they could draw. Duncan followed sweeping the right side of the room. They shot everyone three times to make sure they were dead, twice in the chest and once in the head. Alec shouted, "Clear!"

"All clear!" Duncan replied as they went to the computer. He placed a spider looking hacking device onto the console allowing him access to the computer. He started manipulating holographic images as Lauren came through the door firing away down at the soldiers coming at them from the catwalk. Alec kept his attention on the stairs in front of him. Lauren asked, "How long?"

"Give me a minute!" Duncan snapped as some of the holo-images turned green indicating he was gaining access. Alec was suddenly surprised as he saw a shadow leap down the stairs. In one swift motion, the shadow pulled Alec's weapon from hands and hit him in the face mask, hard. Everything slowed down as he saw a plasma knife being thrust towards his torso. He quickly used his rifle to block the stab. It got cut in half rendering it useless. Alec drew his pistol down as the figure pulled out his own side arm. Both of them aimed at each other at the same time and fired. Alec ducked down dodging the shot while the person slapped Alec's pistol making him miss. The person lower their aim and fired again. Alec's pushed up making the round miss. Alec lunged his weapon forward and fired, aiming for the person's torso. He went forward dodging the round and kneed Alec in the chest. As he went down Lauren leaped forward kicking the person with both of her legs. The person did a back flip and took a shot at Duncan. Lauren used herself as a shield, taking the shot and losing her already damaged arm. Alec fired away at the person, knocking the pistol out of his hands, and hitting him once in the head. The person pulled off his helmet showing its true face. It was a Vegan. His eyes went wide as he seemed do a series of deep croaks. He ran off as Lauren shot at him. Duncan yelled, "Got it!"

The platform suddenly shook as the massive cylinder went down and took aim at the other platforms. "A little taste of their own medicine!"

There was the loud boom again, this time followed by several more. The platform rocked like the ground was shaking. "Hang on!" yelled Lauren.

The room suddenly flipped over and everyone one went flying into the walls with a loud crash. Everything went dark as they laid there for a moment. Alec was the first to get up as he went over to Lauren. She grabbed him pulling herself up. Duncan laughed, "This beach is open for business!"

"Come on. We need to get to the others," Lauren commanded as she leaned on Alec. The three of them went out the door. The whole platform was knocked down from the blast. Only the legs held up the main section and kept it from toppling over completely. Tara, Nick and Mindy walked over still shaking and speechless. "Where's the Falcon?" asked Lauren.

They all looked over at the down craft. It was pinned underneath a growing pile of debris. They all quickly ran over to it, leaping over the dead and the shards of metal. Duncan and Tara ripped their way inside and pulled Bryan and Alisa out. Bryan was now covered in burns, and Alisa had several broken bones. "Fuck you Lauren! Fuck you!" she screamed.

Lauren dropped to the ground. Alec quickly went to her side. "Are you all right?"

"Nothing that a little repairs can't fix," she said as a single tear slid down the still organic side of her face, "We've lost too many."

"We got the job done. We did what we were supposed to do. Look up." Alec pointed at the sky. Several destroyers and transports came down firing away and clearing the Alliance ground personnel. The Transports landed with additional forces spreading out like an infestation. "We did it. We're home," Alec reassured everyone.

They marveled over the sight of so many vessels landing at once. The Alliance was now being routed from the orbital bombardment and the ships that had already landed. Nick got on the radio, "This is Squad Thirteen. Requesting extraction, over."

"So the Vegans finally showed their ugly faces. What now?" Alec asked. Lauren sighed with her voice sounding distorted, "Now things get ever more interesting. At least we have more to kill than just humans."

"That kind of sounds racist," Alec joked. Lauren laughed and sarcastically said, "All you organics are the same to me."

Everyone chuckled as they enjoyed the fireworks.

CHAPTER 12
TEST
UNKNOWN DATE
UNKNOWN LOCATION
PANDORA
INFIRMARY

Alec once again woke up with a headache, in green coveralls, and with Doc hovering over him. "What happened?" Alec asked.

"One unanticipated thing about the warp jump is that it almost killed everyone onboard. If it wasn't for your fake organs and armored suit, you'd be dead," Doctor told him. "Where are we, and how did the explosion almost kill us? I thought the Icarus partials could take out a star," he probed.

"Only if they interact with the right materials. In the form it was in, it just took out a section of the asteroid belt, Pluto mainly. As far as the Alliance is concerned, we're dead. It might have only been minutes here, but it's been eight years for the Sol system"

"What? You've got to be kidding me!" Alec gasped in surprise. Doc explained, "Time is relative. We held still and everything else moved on. Ironic how going fast makes time go slower while staying still makes time fly by."

Alec nodded as he tried to get up, but fell back as his legs gave out on him. His body felt sore as he leaned back sitting on his knees. Doc smiled, "You really shouldn't try getting up too fast. You'll just end up back down again."

Alec looked up at him, annoyed with his constant quips. He stood there tapping away at his data pad. "Everyone in your squad is all right. They're on the mess deck right now if you want to meet them. There's no foreseeable operation coming up, so take some time to rest and relax. With the amount of stress you've had to endure, it might end up killing you."

"Really? I thought getting shot, blown up, and stabbed would get me killed first." Alec got back his my feet adjusting to the gravity and not having an armored suit on. "Injuries can easily be mended. As for mental trauma, not so much," Doc reminded him.

"I'll keep that in mind," Alec replied as he walked out as quickly as he could. He didn't want to hear anything else the doctor had to say. Alec went through the airlock and out into the passageway. Everything seem relaxed for once with the air and gravity still on. It was a welcome to not have to have a suit on. Thankfully the infirmary and the mess decks were right next to each other, along with the galley. As he moved through the food line, Alec thought about how most of his organs were fake. He just stuck to a large bottle of soda. They didn't have beer for some reason, so soda would have to do. He walked into the almost empty mess deck seeing several empty tables with seats attached to them. Along the walls were flat screens that were turned off at the moment. It seemed overly familiar to him. There was only one table occupied with the members of the squad. They were sitting around quietly drinking without looking at each other. All of them were in the same green coveralls and looked groggy. Alec took a seat without any of them looking over at him. "Hi," he said.

Yeager spontaneously stood up and shouted, "Fuck you!"

Kathryn grabbed him and pulled him down, slapping him across the face. "Not now!"

"Well, anyone else have a friendly greeting for me?" Alec asked sarcastically leaning back against the short round metal chair. Mira smiled, "Want some liquor in your drink?"

He thought about it, "Wait, we physically can't get

drunk off of alcohol. We don't have the right organs for that. What's the point?"

She told him, "Flavoring."

He sighed offering up his bottle. She poured some clear booze inside. It did improve the taste of the drink. Alec thanked her.

"Funny how we have a whole area dedicated to food consumption when no one on this ship really needs to eat," Cullen pointed out while eating some chocolate ice cream. He seemed to enjoy it. Alec asked, "Wait, if we can eat, what happens to the food afterwards?"

Cullen explained, "Well seeing how we don't have a real digestive system anymore, we eventually have to throw it up or shit it out."

Alec nodded as it didn't sound any different from normal consumption. Jane went on as she put her hand on Alec's leg underneath the table, "We need little reminders of what it was like to be human. Our bodies might be able to cope with the changes easily, but our minds still need something to help it along. Kind of like how we still have sex drives even though we don't need to reproduce. Have to keep our thoughts stimulated."

Both of them smiled as they looked at each other. Then, Alec had to bring it up, "Well, Kathryn was made for reproduction at least and did it successfully?"

Kathryn's eyes went wide when she heard this. Yeager got even more infuriated than before. He got up with Kathryn holding him back. He yelled, "Don't you ever talk about my mother!"

"Sit down!" Kathryn snapped at him as he took his seat again, clinching his fists while shaking. She looked over at Alec, "No offense taken. I, a mere machine, was able to have life created in my artificial womb. I don't see that as a problem. What I do have an issue with is you trying to goad my son into a fight."

Alec rolled his eyes caving in to his own frustrations, "I'm goading him? You heard what he said when I walked in? So it's cool for him to act like an antagonizing brat, but if I just ask a question I'm the instigator? I got to say, I wish Lauren was still here. She didn't seem to have a double standard like you do!"

This time there wasn't any stopping Yeager. He leaped up into the air and started hitting Alec in the head over and over saying, "Fuck you, Dad!"

When he swung in with his right arm again, Alec moved his head out of the way making him Yeager the wooden floor. Using his own momentum against him, Alec kneed him in the groin and yelled, "I'm not your fucking father!"

Alec suddenly heard laughter from behind him. By

the depth of his voice, Alec knew who it was. "Please don't stop. This is too funny."

Yosemite was crouching down with his head just below the overhead. He still had on his dark armored suit and still had that wide smile showing off his razor sharp teeth. He went over to Yeager, picked him up by the neck and slapped him against the overhead holding him up. He whispered to him and Yeager just responded, "Yes!"

Yosemite dropped him on the deck. Quickly he got back up and walked out the door. "Would you all kindly leave us?" Kathryn asked.

Everyone filed out of the room. Kathryn walked up to Alec, "I miss Lauren, too. I would trade places with her if I could. Also…" She punched Alec in the gut, "Don't ever use her memory against me again!"

She walked out leaving him with Yosemite who asked, "You really have a way with comrades, don't you?"

"What can I say? I'm good at pissing people off… inadvertently." He sighed sitting back down. He took a swig of his drink. It left him longing for the days when alcohol would work the way it was supposed to. Yosemite laughed to himself, "That you are. What do you remember about the past so far?"

"I remember up to the landings on Mars." Yosemite grinned, "Having any experiences with time lapse in your life?"

"No," Alec responded as thought back through some of his recent memories. One thing stuck out in his mind, "How come in the past I shot right handed and now I use my left hand to shoot?"

"Thing change. As long as the memories are coming, we'll have what we want soon enough." He moved his body around with the sound of clanking metal echoing in the room. Alec asked, "So we have a faster than light drive. What now?"

"Now we get ready for the fight to come. Before we leave this system, we'll leave a mark letting them know we'll return. For now, just enjoy the peace. It won't last for long." He told him as he walked out leaving Alec alone. "Creepy bastard," Alec thought to himself.

He walked out the door still hurting from the hits he'd took. Jane was waiting outside for him, "You really have a way with words don't you?"

He looked over at her as she walked up to him. Alec didn't know how she was going to act, "Guess I'm a good instigator. Sorry if I offended you."

"Not yet." She leaned in and kissed him on the lips. He was surprised and relieved at the same time. She went back and Alec smiled, "I think some of that stimulation you mentioned earlier sounds good right about now."

"Couldn't agree more. Follow me." She pulled his hand and Alec followed her down the passageway. It didn't take long before they got to a fan room that was deserted from the rest of the ship. Jane closed the door behind them and changed the images from air units to that of the stars illuminating the room. "I think this will help with the mood," she smiled playfully.

"So will this." Alec went in and kissed her over and over. Both of them started unzipping their coveralls and kicking off their boots. He hugged her, keeping her warm body close to him. Alec closed his eyes and put his focus on the present moment. Both of them lifted each other's shirts off and threw them aside. She pulled off his tank top as Alec undid her bra. Her well rounded breasts made his now artificial heart skip a beat. Whoever made her had good taste. With one hand Alec massaged one of her breasts, noticing the nipple get firmer as he rubbed. With the other hand he pulled her panties down. She slid off his underwear as they kept kissing. Jane grabbed him and guided him inside of her as they leaned against a wall. She felt warm and moist and both were instantly stimulated. He didn't care if what he felt was artificial; it felt good. He went back and forth feeling her constrict around him. Her fingernails dug into his back as he moved his hips into. She moved along with him as they kept kissing to keep her moans from getting too loud.

She jumped on Alec, and he feel backwards. He caught himself with his arms as she bounced up and down. Using his legs, he thrust up as she came down, using one of his hands to rub her. This made her moan louder. Alec stopped caring about the noise as she turned around. He loved the sight of her butt as she arched her back and slid up and down him. The feeling of it as it impacted his body was sensational. He kept thrusting, then pushed forward to her knees. This got the deepest penetration. Alec thrust over and over. She rubbed herself adding to her own stimulation. He leaned forward to kiss her neck and help her rub. She turned over on her back and pulled him down on top of her. As their kisses grew more intense, both of them started to reach their climax. They moved faster and faster until both bodies started shaking as one. He laid on top of her, feeling a release as she gasped. They laid there for a while, but it didn't feel like it would be long enough. Alec rolled next to Jane and hugged her from behind. She turned and wrapped her legs around him. Both of them laid there holding each other as they sighed from the sensations. Alec laughed, "That's one bodily function I'm glad we still get to use."

"It is good to be anatomically correct," Jane smiled tightening her grip on him. Alec might have felt tired afterwards, but he didn't want to fall asleep. He wanted this to last as long as possible. He thought about his recent memories and the other Jane that died in the wreck. Alec held her and said, "I'm not going to lose you."

"I'm easy to find. It will be all right." She kissed him, assuring him that all was well. For the first time in what felt like forever, Alec felt safe. The two of laid there in each other's arms as they looked at the images of stars above. Alec asked, "You ever dream?"

"I can't dream." She looked down with a hint of disappointment. "If you're referring to my goals, I want to be more that what I was made to be."

"I think you succeeded. You literally did more and are more than what you were created to be," Alec reassured her as he massaged her shoulders. This made her smile as she laid her head on his chest. It felt like it had been too long since he felt that feeling. Then the intercom boomed, "All Squad Thirteen members gather in Classroom One."

"Guess recess is over," Jane sighed as she started putting her clothes back on. Alec followed suit but not in any real rush. He asked, "Were we close before?"

"Not back then, but things change. Let get going. Don't want to keep the others waiting," Jane answered. She got dressed really quickly. Alec had to struggle to keep up. She went out the door first. He followed trying to get his boots on, and his coveralls were still unzipped. Alec got out the door and heard a voice call out, "Have fun?"

"Mira?" Alec saw her looking very jealous. "Well?"

He wasn't having it, "Yes, and she didn't stick anything into my eye! I don't want to know what kind of other fetishes you're into."

"You liked everything before that," Mira walked up to him. Jane stepped in between, "He doesn't like you that way. Deal with it."

"How did you like dealing with my sloppy seconds?" Mira snapped at her. Alec stepped back not liking where this was going. Jane shot back, "There wasn't much to deal with seeing how your vagina is as dry as sandpaper!"

Mira threw the first punch hitting Jane in the jaw. She threw a second one, but Jane ducked down and punched her in the ribs three times. Mira kicked Jane in the head knocking her down and leaped on top of her. Jane landed a punch square on her nose, breaking it. Soon the two of them were grappling trying to lock the other in a chokehold. Alec stepped in knowing it wasn't a good idea, "Calm down!"

Kathryn suddenly stepped in and pulled the two of them apart, "So now I can't leave any of you alone without you trying to either kill or screw each other? Damned children!"

"In my defense, she started it!" Jane pointed at Mira as she gave her the finger. "Enough! We are going to be killing good and plenty soon enough. Isn't that enough for you all? And you, why can't you ever keep your pants on?"

Alec got defensive when he heard this, "Really Kathryn? Look who's talking! What did it take for that john to get your pants off? Do you always have such double standards? At least I didn't end up stuck with a bastard!"

The look of rage in her eyes gave him chills. She must have punched Alec in the head because the next things he saw were stars. These weren't holo-images either. They seemed to move rapidly as he fell to the deck like a ton of bricks.

CHAPTER 13
BLOODY OLYMPUS
2211
MARS
LYCUS SULCI
CAMP FRED MILLER

IT was a clear night, and the stars shone brightly. It looked like the whole universe was in view to the eyes below. Also in sight were the raining torpedoes coming down like meteors. All of them had a long steak of light following them as they fell. In the background was the sound of weapons fire still bombing over the horizon. The squad sat on top of a grass covered hilltop where they had a view of Olympus Mons. The mountain glowed with every hit that impacted the energy shield that protected it. The fire flashed as it trickled down the shield. The mountain held against the bombardment. No amount of plasma torpedoes, nuclear missiles, or partial blasts seemed to penetrate the shields. Lauren walked up to the squad as they sat around relaxing their armor while drinking and enjoying the sights. She asked, "Is everyone here? I've got something to tell… wait, where did you get that beer?"

Nick laughed, "We liberated it from a brewery. We need it for war effort!"

"Isn't that going to piss off the locals and hinder their economy?" Lauren asked. Duncan laughed, "After all the hell the androids and clones have been raising, I don't think the economy is going to bounce back any time soon."

"Don't forget about the collateral damage from the bombardment, crashed ships, and fire fights. All in the name of liberty!" Alisa cheered rubbing her repaired face as she drank. Lauren shook her head, "Got another drink?"

Alec threw her one. She opened it with her teeth and joined them as they watched Olympus. The Mech, tanks, artillery and orbital strike still pounded away at the shield. The blast illuminated the mountain as if it were broad daylight. Tara asked, "So Lauren, weren't you going to say something?"

She took a long swig of her drink and stared at the mountain. Alec asked, "Well don't keep us waiting. What is it?"

"The shield's coming down within the next day. Once it does, we're going to be in the first wave," Lauren bluntly told them. Everyone looked at her ignoring the explosions and bombs echoing around them. The new Jane

68 asked, "So what are we riding?"

Lauren sighed after taking another long swig of her drink, "Our feet. That's what we're going to be on."

Bryan got up, still recovering from his injuries and snapped, "This is bullshit! Why the hell do we have to start from the bottom? Also how come Jane got a new body, and I'm stuck with the one that got smashed?"

Jane grabbed him by the throat, "Sorry if my old body got completely splattered by the fucking crash! Next time I'll try harder to only get partly crushed like you did!"

"Wait, I thought you were just a replica of…" Alisa was about to ask, but she got cut of when Jane slapped her across the face. "Don't any of your jerk wads listen? I explained it earlier!"

"In our defense, we were sober earlier," Tara told her finishing her drink. Lauren went over and grabbed her arm to calm her down. She explained, "Every clone and AI has a link to a memory bank. So in case one dies, the memories go to the next body. So I remember the fucking agony of being fucking killed!"

"Wait, why couldn't we bring Fred back then?" Mindy got up while trying not to fall back down. Lauren explained, "Because normal organics aren't linked to the system."

Jane interjected, "You assholes couldn't handle

being killed!"

"I think that goes for most living things. I mean when has death been easy to handle?" Nick asked while opening another bottle. Lauren sighed breaking out the pills that would instantly sober them up, "Save this for when we have to move out. We'll have to be on standby here hours in advance."

"Hurry up and wait?" Duncan asked. Lauren nodded, "Always. Some things don't change over the years. On the flip side, we'll have armored support, closed in artillery, air support, and even orbital support. We'll all have on juggernaut armor on top of our Iron Clad suits. Yet like every well defeated mountain, this is going to suck."

"How much fight could they have after being under siege for all these months?" Bryan asked. Lauren kept explaining, "We'll find out soon enough. One more round and after that we have to start moving to the front."

Everyone finished the drinks they had and quickly grabbed another as they looked on with horror and anticipation at the mountain. Alec asked, "So Mindy, why did you join in?"

She sighed, "They offered me a cure for the cancer I had. I couldn't afford it because I was homeless."

"How did you end up with cancer and homeless?"

Alisa asked. Mindy drank some more altering the way she was sitting down. Mindy explained, "When I was in the Alliance Navy I worked on some hazardous partials. It was supposed to be some revolutionary shit. Unfortunately for us, the Vegans didn't like what we were doing. They staged an accident, and only a few of us survived. They blamed us for what happened."

"Wait, you survived the Icarus Incident?" Tara interrupted. Mindy nodded, "Yeah. We named the damned partial after that ship. I think it was named after an ancient something or other. Well, we got blamed and kicked out like yesterday's garbage. I trusted them. Never felt so betrayed in my life. After that, I did what all other homeless people did, live out in the forest."

"I didn't know there still were homeless. Why didn't you go to a shelter?" Nick asked. Mindy took another swig of her drink, "People just don't want to deal with us, kind of like how they don't want to deal with criminals, warriors, and artificial life. They don't want their perfect little existence to be bothered. I hope the assholes living it up in their damned towers got a rude awakening when we landed. Can't wait to go to Earth and do it all again."

"I think we'd all love to do it again," Bryan smiled thinking about it. The others looked over. Jane asked,

"What did you do again before all this?"

Bryan answered, "I was… a prostitute." Everyone started laughing. Duncan said in between gasps, "Bullshit!"

Lauren laughed like never before. She said, "He's telling the truth. Kathryn recruited him while she was undercover."

This made them laugh even harder. Alec gasped, "People wanted to pay you for your body?"

"I looked like this before I joined the Corps! Unlike you out of shape assholes, I worked for this body! I didn't need any fucking augmentation!"

"Not what Kathryn and my sister told me," Jane said. Bryan insecurely snapped, "So what if I was a clone? Augmentation and pills are not the same thing!"

Nick patted him on the shoulder, "Can't get it naturally, don't deserve it."

"That's rich coming from a guy who used to be a dwarf!" He snapped back at him. Nick argued, "Five foot nine inches isn't that short!"

"The average height of a normal male is six feet five inches. You kind of sound like a shrimp in more ways than one," Alisa pointed out while winking. He snapped, "I didn't fuck my way up the chain in prison by being a shrimp!"

"You could have used random object to do your dirty work," Bryan tapped him on the back. Nick replied, "I did what I did for dominance! You got paid to bend over!"

"Currency gives me a hard on. I only demonized people if that's what they wanted unlike you sick bastard. Don't judge me. Like I said, I got paid! By people!" Bryan put a lot of emphasis on being paid. Tara bluntly asked, "How did a man whore like you end up in the Corps?"

"Got paid to." Bryan told them quickly and with sincerity. Alec got up, "How come this asshole gets paid, and we don't?"

"He got paid with medicine," Lauren told everyone. Bryan looked over, "I was doing a good enough job telling my business on my own. Don't help!"

"Not like it matters," Jane finished her drink. Nick asked, "What's that supposed to mean?"

"Why keep secrets if we're all more than likely about to get killed soon? Think about it. It doesn't matter what we all know about each other, because we might not live to see tomorrow," Jane grabbed another drink and took a long swig. Alisa huffed, "Thanks for being so uplifting. We're having a good time making fun of man whore and prison rape while getting hammered, and you have to bring up death again."

"Do you all not see that fucking mountain?" she pointed at the particle blast impacting into the shields. It seemed that slowly but surely the energy shield was going down. "Forgive me if I'm concerned about getting killed again!"

"We're all concerned about getting killed once. Twice on the other hand..." Mindy paused. As Lauren stepped up, "We're going, like it or not. Our ride will be here soon."

"Wait, I thought you said we weren't getting a ride?" Nick asked as a Crain came swooping over them. As it hovered, Lauren told them, "I didn't say we had to walk to the mountain. We do have to climb eventually. Take your pills. You don't want to fly drunk."

All of them got up putting their armored suits back to normal wear and picking up their weapons. The grass genially moved with the wind and the pressure from the transport. One by one, they filed inside. There were several others crammed in the Crain donning Juggernaut suits on top of their Iron Clad armor, too. It was reminiscent of the deep sea diver suits of old. Both of them are meant to take abuse. One difference is that the Juggernaut suits had a rocket launcher and a machine gun on their backs.

Each of them stepped back letting the armor wrap around their suits. It only took seconds before it was fully donned. Lauren motioned for everyone to gather around her. The Crain seemed to be shaking more than usual. It must have been from the nearby bombardment. Everyone had to hold on as the craft moved randomly. Inside, other squads were gathering around their team leaders getting ready for what was to come. A hologram of the mountain came into view. The sides even had slopes going diagonally up the mountain. There was an incline that went from sea level to about forty nine thousand feet high. That wasn't even the peak of the mountain. On the western side were all the cities, on the east was just desert. Olympus City was geared towards attracting tourist to the beaches and the mountain. It didn't hurt that it was next to one of the largest military bases in the system, the headquarters for the Alliance. It truly was a fortress.

On the very top of the mountain were the communications antennas. Spread out around the mountain were shield generators. The amount of power that had to go into keeping it up must have been massive. The whole mountain was about the size of France. Along with shields, it had several thousand turrets, anti-air launchers, and pillboxes though out, not to mention the mines probably on the mountain, too. The hologram showed us the tunnel network they had. It was extensive to say the least. Around the mountain appeared images of the troops moving in from every side and direction.

Lauren briefed them, "Our objective is to secure the hanger by the eastern side of the mountain. When the shield goes down, we'll dust off on top of the plateau. Once we do, we'll have to go sixty two miles just to make it to the hangers. The only cover we'll have is the smoke clouds we'll be deploying ahead of time. We might be blind, but so will they. We'll have vehicles that come with us, along with air and orbital support. We're going into a wasp's nest of defenders. I think you all see what we're dealing with. Any questions?"

"Why couldn't we just dust off right on top of the hanger itself?" Mindy asked. Lauren explained, "There will be forces dropping in like that, just not us. Besides, those squadrons are going to get cut to pieces. You really want to be a part of that?"

"Explain to me how we're the vanguard again when others go first?" Nick wondered out loud. Lauren told him, "Because we are the first of the main forces, not the main cannon fodder groups. We're still part of the tip of the spire, just not the lead point."

"So we're going to get the shaft?" Alec asked. Lauren sighed again, "Not as badly as others. A lot of people today are going to get shafted, us included. Our only focus is to get to the hanger. Other units will take care of the defenses. We only deal with them if we have to. Any other questions?"

"If we have to be fast, why are we wearing the extra armor and having to rely on armored vehicles?" Bryan asked with fear in his voice. Lauren seemed to look around before she answered, "They're only going to last us up to a point. We'll have good and plenty of distance to shed weight. I also should have mention this earlier. Try not to get a puncture in your suit. It's going to be cold, the air is going to be thin and the wind will be blowing hard. Any other questions?"

Alisa asked, "Is there anything else we're missing or that we should know about? We really should have put a little more preparation into this."

"When we are left with no cover besides craters and debris, we move on all fours. Stay close to the ground and only move when the smoke clouds are the thickest. Save your hand held weapons for when we get close. One way or another, this mountain is going to fall. We're going in for our landing soon. These Alliance assholes think they are being heroic. Let's kill them."

"Hell yeah," Duncan said with fear and a strange hint of glee in his voice. He reached over grabbing Alec's shoulder, "This mountain can suck our genitals."

"So can the wind, cold and air pressure," Alec said

while nodding. Everyone started touching as they huddled up. Tara got so enthusiastic she yelled, "Physical pressure for us all!"

Everyone seemed to roll with it. Jane laughed, "Everyone but the Alliance assholes."

Lauren broke up the huddle, "Yes. Great, motivation aside, get ready to dust off."

She and the rest of the team gathered near the doors. As what seemed like a cruel joke there was a timer above the opening. It counted down from one minute. To everyone one looking at it, time seemed to go way too fast. The team gripped their rifles either at the high or the low ready. All of them made sure not to sweep each other with their muzzles. Alec got his breathing under control and only heard the vibration of the Crain as it lowered down. The light went green and time was up. The doors opened and everyone rushed out. They ran out into the cold, snow covered ground. The wind was blowing against them as they moved forward. Next to them, the armored corps was coming up. There was a long line of hover tanks staying low to the ground, and next to them were the giant Mechs. They didn't have any problem climbing the mountain. From above came hundreds of fighters and transports moving in as fast as possible. The fighters pounded the mountain with bombs and missiles making the ground shake. Even though the shield was down, the mountain wasn't going down easily. The Alliance turrets started making life hell for anyone up in the air. They fired out torpedoes and missiles that detonated in the air and focused all the shrapnel and explosive force upward. This caused debris to hail down. One shard came down right on top of the Crain as it was taking off. This made it spiral out of control down over the mountain. Alisa's voice screamed over the radio, "You're telling me we have to walk through this shit?"

"Would you rather be in the air?" Jane pointed at what looked like a fireworks show flashing above. Lauren led the way, "This mountain isn't getting any smaller. If it does, we'll be in trouble."

"I think we already are," Nick pointed up at the sky as an Eagle came down, dropping like a brick. They rushed out of the way as it smashed behind him. The explosion didn't produce too much heat since everything this high was frozen. They started moving from cover to cover as fast as they could while the sun came up in the sky. The stars disappeared as the sky turned blue with pillars of black smoke rising all over. The crafts up above could only be seen in the sky when they were hit. Squad Thirteen and several others moved at a good pace to the mountain's summit. All of them were able to keep sprinting, even up an incline, when one operative suddenly flew backwards with part of his head missing. Someone shouted, "Snipers!"

Everyone ducked down, but not before ten more operatives got hit. Hitting the ground and laying down didn't help. Not even the massive amounts of smoke helped. There was little to take cover behind. The rounds only made a sound after they hit. By then, someone was already down. The tanks fired back on where they thought the snipers were hiding, as did the Mechs. The armored unit in front of the operatives provided cover and fire support. That's when they started running into mines. One blast was strong enough to send a tank flying in the air before landing upside down. Any operators unlucky enough to be nearby died from the blast. They looked like they were hit by a vehicle afterwards. After that came the mortar attacks. They rained down super-heated plasma. Shrapnel burst, cutting apart anything and anyone who didn't have strong enough shielding. People's bodies were diced apart, cauterized and frozen within seconds. The Spartans kept grinding forward even as the fire got worse as they went along. Bryan asked, "We've only covered twenty miles in one hour? This is bullshit!"

"Who said this was going to be quick?" Lauren replied, "At least all of us still have our juggernaut suits intact." Just as Lauren said that, an artillery round slammed right into her chest and cut her head clean off. The round was a dud, but it did its damage. The others rushed around her head. It fell out of her helmet, but she still showed signs of life. Lauren asked in a distorted voice, "Would one of you kindly pick me up?"

"How are you still alive?" Duncan asked, amazed by the sight. She snapped, "Pick me the fuck up! It's cold down here!"

Alec grabbed her head and held it like a ball. She screamed, "Keep moving!"

"I've heard of headless people, but never a bodiless person," Tara commented as they came under automatic weapons fire. Lauren shouted, "Almost there, just a few more miles."

"What's a few?" Alec asked as he ducked down missing a sniper's bullet. As it snapped above him she said, "Just forty miles more."

"One third of the way? This is bullshit!" Jane snapped as she huddled behind a tank. A loud bomb echoed from above. They looked out, seeing one of the Mechs get hit. It fell right next to them with a loud thud. A hover tank went over it and fired back. Above, the transports and fighters were still getting chewed up by the anti-air flak being sent at them. Slowly yet surely, the turrets were being taken out. Despite the casualties, there wasn't anything stopping the momentum of the Spartans. They got closer, under more heavy fire, but according to their global positioning systems, almost to the hangers. Bryan cheered, "Almost fucking there!"

A shrapnel burst exploded behind him and he suddenly went down face first. The others quickly rushed to him as they pulled him to cover behind a burning tank. Bryan was screaming over and over again. He took a sniper round that took down his shielding, sending several large shards of shrapnel in his back. It went from red to black as they embedded themselves in his spine. "Give him some pain killers so he doesn't die!"

Mindy stuck him with some pain killers, but it didn't help him much. Jane even said, "That has to hurt."

"The follow up forces will take care of him. We have to keep going!" Lauren egged them on. Reluctantly, they left Bryan with only a beacon as they moved forward. They were almost there, seeing the summit in full view in front of them. They kept passing by burned out pillboxes and dead bodies. No Alliance soldiers were being taken prisoner to say the least. They didn't have much further to go, yet the fire intensified. The air forces finally made progress by delivering extra payloads on top of the defenders. For a second, it looked like all the defenses went down. Those that got carried away were in for a shock. The hanger bay doors opened and every fighter the Alliance had left along with a swarm of missiles came flying out. "Incoming!" yelled Nick.

One missile landed right in front of the squad knocking everyone down. Nick, Jane and Mindy's juggernaut suits were trashed and had to be peeled off. Duncan let out a cry that pierced through the hailstorm of weapons fire. Alec ran up to him and gasped. His whole lower body was ripped off leaving only his burned torso. The wound was cauterized and frozen, so it kept him breathing. He grabbed Alec and moaned, "Kill me!"

Lauren snapped, "You can get a new cock and balls after this! Don't wuss out over losing your old ones. Place a beacon on him and keep moving!"

They didn't have much choice in the matter. At this point, they were crawling on all fours and constantly ducking down to dodge runs from the enemy fighters or weapons fire from the hanger. At least they were in position to fire back. Their back mounted machine guns and rocket launchers gave them comfort as they fired. It helped them move forward. One enemy Hawk fighter came swooping in. Jane got up firing away. A lucky rocket scored a hit on the cockpit, and the fighter went crashing down, shattering to pieces. "Hell…"

Jane fell backwards with a bullet hole in her helmet. The others stood still for a second as they looked at her limp body lying in the snow. Lauren encouraged them, "Let's hurt these bastards and hurt them very much."

Once again, they moved forward, using incendiary rounds on the enemies. It only took a single hit for their target to catch fire and burn slowly if the round got in touch with their flesh. Lauren seemed to take great joy in watching this. They were almost at the doors of the hanger bay. They could see inside and see the prize. Then, in front of them, several mines went off, stopping them cold. This time Tara screamed as she crawled on her back holding what was left of her arms. Nick placed a beacon on her, and they moved on. The remaining team made one last mad dash to the corner of the door while still under fire. Several operatives with them were dropping like flies as they ran. They formed up next to the door getting ready to storm inside. The ground vehicles that were still working laid down cover fire and gave live feeds of what they were going into. Squad by squad, they went around the corner and charged inside. It came time for Thirteen's turn. Alisa was in front and about to signal them to advance when suddenly the part of the door she was standing behind blew up, sending her backwards. Nick and Mindy grabbed her and pulled her to the wall. She was grabbing her stomach as her lower torso looked like it was ripped apart. This time at least she was attended by medics. Alec looked at the squad and saw it was only him, Mindy, Nick and Lauren's severed head left, "Shit! I can't believe only a few of us made it!"

"I can't believe the Alliance has more powerful weapons now!" Mindy interjected. Lauren, still in charge, told them, "They were going to adapt eventually! Now get inside and kill them!"

The three of them still had their juggernaut suits mostly intact, which would give them a fighting chance. The back mounted weapons came over their shoulders as they prepped to go in. They waited for a plasma round to fly inside and blow up. Alec went first running towards the nearest cover he saw. The others operatives were leap frogging their way inside from cover to cover. Anyone who was holding a position laid down cover fire for the rest. Inside looked like a bee hive with hundreds of octagons that would normally have contained spacecraft or aircraft in them. Instead there were just tools and boxes laying all over the place along with dead defenders and barricades. Some of them were nothing more than mechanics armed with small pistols. They never stood a chance.

The three of them ran over the dead to the first door they saw, ready to gain access to the complex itself.

Before they could get to it, the door exploded, sending them backwards. They were able to get back up again while shedding their destroyed Juggernaut armor. They pulled their assault rifles off their backs and rushed through the door. All lights were off, leaving them in the dark. They activated their night vision as they went in. The hull looked to be caving in from all the bombardments it had probably taken. They heard a loud buzzing sound and saw a flashing light, "Oh shit!"

They were all blinded by the flash leaving them vulnerable. Nick suddenly let out a muffled cry as it looked like he was grabbed. Alec and Mindy chased after him. Whoever had him was fast and managed to stay one step ahead of them. Nick's voice came over the radio, "They got me! I can't break free!"

"We're coming for you! Hang on!" Alec shouted as they kept trying to catch up. Eerily, Nick seemed to calm down, "He's leading you into a trap! Don't come after me!"

"We can handle anything that asshole has for us!" Mindy exclaimed, trying to keep his spirits up. Nick suddenly grunted. They could hear him groaning. Nick uttered out, "Don't die here!"

The communication then went dead. Lauren shouted at them, "It's a trap! Nick is gone! We need to regroup with someone else!"

"I'm not giving up on him!" Mindy shouted. She kept going. Alec tried to stop her, "Wait!"

They both ran through a door with a mine waiting for them. Mindy went backward using her body to shield Alec as it went off. The two of them were knocked down by the blast. Alec got up first. He couldn't see at all. A shard of shrapnel was stuck in his eyes, keeping him blind. He frantically felt around and found Mindy. Alec felt burning metal and smelled it, too. He felt cold and had a hard time breathing. Mindy grabbed his hand. Alec jumped at first, then leaned in, "Mindy?"

"It's okay," she whispered to him through the pain, "I have my boots on, and I wasn't doomed to get stuck in a bed in the end. This was more fulfilling…"

"You'll be fine! We'll get a medic!" Alec tried to reassure her, when he was really trying to reassure himself. Mindy rasped, "I am fine… I am…"

Her hand dropped down to the deck. Alec stepped back as Lauren snapped, "Stop! You'll go over a catwalk!"

"What?" he stopped moving, feeling the wind flow around him. Lauren ordered, "They must have had a getaway vehicle. Hold my head in one hand and use your sidearm with the other. We need to get you out of here if we're going to make it."

Alec slowly got up holding Lauren's head like a

lantern as she guided him, "Go five steps forward."

He quietly cried from the pain and loss of his friends as he moved in the dark. "Turn left and keep going until I tell you to stop."

Alec moved forward waving his pistol around trying to feel the wall. He tread lightly making sure he didn't trip over anything. "Stop!"

He held still as Lauren flat out yelled at him, "Fire!"

Alec franticly pulled the trigger over and over not knowing who or what he was shooting at. "To the right, left, down, up!" she commanded.

He ran out of ammo and reloaded quickly using his muscle memory. "Move back!"

Alec stepped back when he felt vibrations on the ground and heard footsteps. He waited for a long pause and then fired every round he had while gripping the pistol tightly. He heard a moan as footsteps sounded like they were running away from them. "He's running away!" Alec said relieved.

"Hope he doesn't survive his damned wounds. Take us back," Lauren told Alec. He moved forward, still being guided by Lauren. There was a rowing noise of what sounded like a transport taking off. It almost drowned out Lauren as he limped forward. Step by step he felt more lightheaded. Just as he felt like giving up, he heard other footsteps. Alec dropped to his knees and laughed. He didn't hear what Lauren was saying. He didn't care. He just waited for what was to come.

CHAPTER 14
RAID
2222
SOL SYSTEM
ORBIT OF PLUTO
CRAIN TRANSPORT

ALEC woke up. He was again in an Iron Clad suit sitting inside a cargo compartment with the rest of his team. Yeager seemed overly happy for once, "So I shot him in the face! Not only did the head vanish, but his torso split in half. His legs even took a couple steps before falling over! Can you believe that shit?"

Alec looked at him wondering how this conversation came up. Even though he had on his skeleton face mask, he could tell Yeager had a smile underneath. Alec uttered, "Not really."

"Neither could I! It's amazing the ways bodies react to being shot!" Alec nodded trying to back away from him. "Yeah... a lot of screaming and bleeding."

"Not if the wounds are cauterized! Got to love

plasma rounds! They make the flesh burn!" Yeager said happily. Alec scooted back in his seat as far he could, still nodding. He discreetly tried to undo his harness to get away. Yeager asked, "Why so antsy?"

"Why are you such a psycho?" Alec got his harness off and floated away from him. Yeager looked at him as he drifted off. Jane grabbed him and pulled him next to her, "You're going to need to strap in."

Alec quickly put on the harness when he asked, "What is going on?"

"You're were…" she paused mid-sentence thinking before she said, "…asleep when we got you onboard. There wasn't enough time to have you part of the brief, so here's a short version of what's going on. We're starting another grind by taking over Pluto," Jane started to explain to Alec as the transport suddenly rocked. It must have just launched from the hanger. "Pluto? What does that rock have?" Alec asked.

"Just a couple observation outposts and a dry dock. We're mostly using it as a diversion to attract the Alliance's attention away from the core worlds." The Crain rocked again, mostly from weapons fire. Alec asked, "Why didn't we have juggernaut suits?"

"We need to be more nimble. Just follow the rest of us. We're coming in for a hot landing." The Crain shock violently and everyone felt a suddenly thud as they impacted against something. A green light went off as everyone got up. There was a little amount of gravity, but not much. It kept everyone on the ground as the teams gathered around a circular hatch that went down. Cullen and Mira opened it up, pulling the lid off and exposing a gray wall with a large hole burned into it. Kathryn and Yeager went down first into the passageway, "Clear."

"All clear" was spoken, and the others dropped in two by two. Alec went down with Jane as they leaped inside. The square shaped passageways had no light and dust floating around. Alec switched his vision seeing several dead laying on the deck. Most of them looked like they suffocated from the breach while clawing at the blast doors. Cullen and Mira went forward placing charges on the door. Everyone else lined up against the bulkhead clearing the center of the passageway. Alec grabbed the SMG off of his chest, loosening the strap while taking care not to sweep the person in front of him. Everyone was armed for close quarters combat having weapons meant for the task. Even Yeager was armed with only a regular shotgun instead of the cannon he normally carried around. Cullen and Mira moved back as everyone ducked down. There wasn't any warning when the charge went off. Everyone felt a thumping motion as part of the door came flying next to them and down the hull as air flowed violently out the hole. Kathryn and Yeager went to the door and threw grenades inside, "Flash bang!"

A bright flash came from the hole in the door. Jane pulled Alec along as they went for the opening. Both of them gathered on opposite sides of the breach. She went in first sweeping the right side. Alec went in second covering the left. He leaped sweeping his weapon from the center of the room to the left. Suddenly right in front of him was a soldier aiming a shotgun right at his head. He went forward dodging the shot, shoving the muzzle of his weapon into the person's chest and pulling the trigger. The auto fire didn't produce much recoil as five rounds were fired off. One of the rounds went all the way though the person coming out the other side. Other Alliance soldiers came around the corner in front of Alec. He ducked down using the dead body as a shield. He kept his weapon shoved inside the wound he'd created and fired back at them. Alec moved forward as the rounds impacted the body in front of him. It felt like holding a punching bag. Jane came up from behind Alec while ducking down, too. She leaned out to pick them off one by one, using Alec as her own shield. As he pushed forward, one soldier was still clinging to life right next to Alec. He aimed at him first and fired. One of the rounds took off all the fingers on the soldier's right hand before hitting him in the face. Alec lost track of the body as it went down, exposing him to the enemy. Quickly he laid down with several partial rounds flying overhead. He still used the dead person as cover while firing back at them. The partial round tore apart the body sending burning shards of metal and flesh up back at Alec. Jane yelled, "Frag out!"

The grenade hit a soldier right in the head before going off. The precision ripped the person's limbs off his body and knocked down the others around them. Alec got up almost slipping in the blood pool he was in and ran to the opposite side of the passageway with Jane right behind him. Alec shouted, "Frag out!"

He blindly threw it around the corner when he felt the grenade impact someone's chest plate. Alec pushed himself back into Jane going backward as it went off. His hand cleared the corner saving him from the blast. Both of them got back up as Yeager and Kathryn leaped around the corner firing away. The two of them joined in. Alec almost slipped on a severed leg. He saw a massive blood streak on the deck with a head and two arms further down the passageway. The others that were knocked down by the blast were soon cut down by plasma fire. Mira and Cullen went forward as the rest followed them in. The path seemed clear as they kept moving forward. Alec followed the arrow guide in his eyes like a dog would chase a car. Next to him was a clear view of the rock planet as well as Neptune and the dwarf world of Charon. They floated perfectly with the other stars glowing around them. They all disappeared from view as Alec rounded a corner.

He froze when in front of him he saw what could only be described as a monster. It was almost as tall as he was, covered in silver armor that looked like saggy skin. Its face mask had two black eyes wide apart. A thin mouth that barely showed interconnecting jagged teeth went across its face. It has a bat like nose, elongated fingers and toes, and it stood hunched over. The artificial hair on Alec's back felt like it was standing up as he felt a kick to his stomach. He went backwards onto the deck as the thing threw a grenade at Mira. Jane leaped forward and swung her SMG like a club hitting the round object back at the alien. Alec leaped forward, using his own body to shield her from the blast. When the grenade went off, his back felt like it had been burned all over. The two of them flew forward down the passageway. Alec landed on top of her with his joints feeling stretched. His back felt like it was on fire.

It took Alec what felt like the longest minute to get back up. He saw the alien was still alive and knocking the others around like rag dolls. Mira had her head shoved into the bulkhead, Cullen got kicked in the facemask, Kathryn got shot in the chest and Yeager got head butted, knocking him down on his back. Jane and Alec both fired back at the alien. A couple hits landed on the left arm and leg. The alien reached down, grabbed Yeager by the foot and lifted him up. They paused their fire as Yeager got kick right towards them. He went right into Alec, knocking him back down on his already hurting back. He pushed him off as he saw Jane firing back at the alien. She ran out of ammo for her main weapons and switched to her secondary while leaping up at the alien. She shoved her pistol into its head while the alien shoved a weapon into her stomach. Both fired at the same. The alien's head was jerked to the side leaving a dent in the helmet. Jane fell lifeless on her back. Yeager and Alec got up and ran towards them. Cullen helped Mira up as she rubbed her helmet. Kathryn got up with sparks flying out of her wounds. Alec went down next to Jane as he read her vital signs. Her air was leaking out faster than his was and it looked like her heart rate was getting weaker. Alec picked her up in his arms and asked franticly, "Where's the nearest air tight compartment?"

Cullen and Yeager grabbed the sleeping alien, and Kathryn lead the way with Mira next to her. Alec ran as fast as he could while carrying her. He ignored the weapons fire around them as they ran into the occasional

Alliance stragglers. Alec looked back wondering why they were dragging along the thing that just tried to kill them. Alec ran up to a set of open doors and closed them once they were inside. The airlock soon filled with air and the other set of doors opened up. Kathryn and Mira charged into the abandoned infirmary. Cullen and Yeager used what they could to strap the alien down in a chair. Lauren leaned against the bulkhead taking off parts of her armor. Alec shouted, "Mira, get me a defibrillator!"

"Okay, hold on." She started looking around the medical equipment as Alec took off parts of Jane's armored suit exposing her torso. The monitor indicated her heart had stopped and she wasn't breathing. Alec pulled up on the clothing beneath exposing her skin, put his hands together on her chest, keeping his arms straight and pushed up and down over and over. After thirty compressions he ripped off her facemask and took off his own. Alec lifted her head and chin while putting his lips against hers. He saw her chest rise with each breath. Alec went back up and kept giving compressions. Mira came up next to him with a red and white box with the word defibrillator on it. She placed the two pads on Jane's chest and yelled, "Clear!"

It sent a charge that made Jane gasp and cough. Mira and Alec laid her on her side allowing her to recover.

Alec laughed, "You're going to be okay."

She smiled while looking up at him. The two of them grasped each other's hands and looked into each other's eyes. Kathryn ordered while attending to her own wounds, "Cullen, tend to Jane. Alec and Mira, over here."

Alec walked over to the bound person as Yeager pulled its helmet off. The alien was Vegan. It made a loud choking sound as she struggled against the restraints on her limbs. Her round black eyes seemed to be scowling at them. Kathryn ordered, "Mira, introduce us."

She punched her across her plain face. The Vegan then laughed, "You punch like a child!"

"You can communicate. That's good. Now despite your smack talking, this can go one of two ways. You can be honest and live, or you can be an asshole and suffer. So first question, are you the only Vegan operative on this station?"

"Is it true that you can remove your own vagina and clean out all the infected cum?" Mira punched her again in the head. She spat out some green blood and looked up at Mira, "I almost felt that one. Almost."

Kathryn finished patching her wounds together and grabbed the defibrillator and attached the pads to the Vegans head. "Let's see how much charge we can get out of this."

Kathryn activated it as the Vegan made a loud choking sound as she violently shock. She was huffing and puffing as she looked down at her with rage. "Are there other Vegan agents on Pluto?"

"Are you a real person?" the alien asked. Kathryn smiled while shocking her again. "Why are you here?"

"To give your mother… wait you don't have a mother. Kind of hard to believe an abomination like you could be one, even if your spawn is a sin against nature." Kathryn kept her smile and shocked her again. The alien laughed as she looked over at Alec then went quiet. She stared at him with surprise in her eyes, "Wait, Petty Officer Calvin Mar…?!"

Suddenly Alec blacked out for what felt like only a second. When he came to he saw he'd shot the Vegan in the head. Kathryn stood up and shouted, "What the hell?"

Alec looked down at his pistol seeing the steam rising from the muzzle end. His eyes were wide as he gasped, "I don't know!"

"Damned moron!" Kathryn kicked the chair sending the dead alien on the deck. Alec holstered his pistol as he stepped backwards. He asked, "What's wrong with me. She had information. Why would I act on impulse like that?"

"Maybe a part of you didn't want to hear what she

knew. It doesn't matter anymore," Kathryn said as Yeager went up to her, "What do you mean, she could have…"

She interrupted and pulled him close. Kathryn said something to him that made him agree with her, "Oh… never mind then."

"Well, being that first things are last now, is the station secure?" Cullen asked covering the entrances. Mira gave the thumbs up, "Station is secure. The other teams are wrapping up as we speak."

"Great. The Pandora is coming in to dock. Let's head back over to welcome her." Kathryn went for the door followed by the others. Alec crouched down and picked up Jane in his arms. He was about to leave when he looked down at the dead Vegan. She'd written a message for him in her own blood, "They lie."

After seeing the message, Alec heard Kathryn yell, "Come on!"

Looking back he saw he had stepped on the writings. Alec quickly walked out of the infirmary as other members of the Sparta Crops roamed the passageways and follow on teams went past them. Alec stayed behind the others as he thought about what the Vegan said and wrote to him. She knew him. The way she talked to him seemed more personal than just a normal nemesis. Had they at least talked before? Jane reached up hugging him, "Thank you."

"Anytime," Alec smiled down at her. She closed her eyes smiling, too. He saw out through one of the windows the Pandora coming in for docking. For as massive as she was, she was nimble.

At the right angle she looked like a four sided star. The square shaped cage was surprisingly able to accommodate the ship. Soon the Pandora was held in place with cables and contactors. In the mirror, something caught his attention. What should have been his reflection wasn't. Alec saw someone else. This man had a scar across his head going from eye to eye. His hair had a red tint, and his eyes were gold instead of brown. The chin had a slit down the middle that was unfamiliar. The nose was wider, and his skin was darker, too. The man in the mirror seemed to be looking at Alec as he winked. Suddenly, everything faded to black.

Chapter 15
2212
Recovery
Mars
Olympus City
Ocean View Hotel

ALEC woke up and climbed out of bed. He lifted his head as he pushed himself up, having a hard time seeing clearly. His new eyes were still adjusting. Tara tapped him on the shoulders, "Either it's room scurvies, or we're too loud for our neighbors."

"What?" Alec heard the loud knocking on the door, and he rolled out of bed in an almost panic. He heard Lauren's voice, "Open the fucking door!"

"Only time that bitch comes around is to give us another damned mission!" Tara grumbled to herself covering her ears with her new arms. Alec crawled to the door barely able to get up. It opened with Lauren standing there with her arms crossed looking down on them, "Guess your hearing is just fine. Vision on the other hand…"

"Do you mind?" Alec said as he fell back down again. Lauren sighed, "Overdoing the painkillers again?"

"Overdoing your authority?" Alec rolled over and smiled at her. She reached down and grabbed him by the throat and pulled him up to his feet. As he gasped for air, she force fed him a pill. It sobered him up as soon as it touched his tongue. Lauren grasped his mouth as she squeezed, "You've had plenty of time to recover, not to mention enough pills to put out a damned whale! You two have nothing to complain about. Hell, Jane died twice, while Alisa and Duncan both lost their original fucking genitals! I lost my fucking original genitals! You do not have it that bad!"

"She had a point there," Tara sighed looking down at herself. Alec mumbled, "How's the new one working for you?"

She slammed him flat against the floor knocking the wind out of him, "Do you see?"

"I felt it..." Alec mumbled as she increased pressure on his mouth, "Your vision. Can you see?"

He nodded. She let go of him allowing him to roll over on his side. Lauren gave Tara a pill, "Be down in the lobby in a half hour."

She walked out with the door slamming behind her. Tara cried at the noise, "I don't want to do this anymore!"

"I don't think any of us do! That last battle sucked! Who would have thought war would suck so hard?" Alec rolled over into the fetal position. Tara rocked back and forward holding the pill in her hands, "I was talking about sobering up. That last battle, we won, right? How come it feels like a loss?"

"We lost people and body parts..." Alec cringed at the thought. Tara whimpered, "This fake arm does nothing for the phantom pains!"

"I think you need to take that sobriety pill now," Alec said while rocking back and forth himself. Tara snapped, "I'm not talking about hallucinations! I feel itching sensations on my arms and they shouldn't itch being fake! Do you know how much it sucks having an itch that can't be scratched?"

"Not really. I do it myself if I have to," Alec reached up rubbing his artificial eyes. Tara moaned as she got out of bed, "I don't think we're thinking about the same thing... ah fuck it. Let's just go."

"Isn't it too late to quit?" Alec wondered out loud. Tara gave him an answer, "I'm the one that's still technically wasted and you're the one misinterpreting. No shit it's too late to quit! They literally own our body parts!"

Alec sat up accepting his situation, "Okay! I get it.

I don't want to lose them… again."

"Come on." Tara threw him some clothing, and they both got dressed in civilian wear. They went down in the elevator to the almost vacant lobby. Only other person there was the hotel desk manager. Lauren called all of them, "Good. For a second there I thought I would have to drag you two out. Let's go."

She led them outside. It was cold and snowing. The snow was thick enough where only part of the skyscrapers were visible. Thankfully, they didn't have to stand outside too long. Once the pill shaped hover bus pulled up to the curb, all of them jumped in. It was warm and roomy inside. Once everyone was in, the bus started driving towards Olympus Mons. The mountain grew in their view as they traveled towards the massive rock. All of them sat there quietly. None of them liked the sight of the mountain after the hell they went through to conquer it. Everyone still had the mental scars of the trauma they endured. All of them were looking in random directions keeping quiet as they sat. Alec broke the silence asking, "Where are we going next?"

"We're going to be training for the next operation," Lauren told him as she lit up a smoke. Tara got defensive saying, "More training! Just because we've been in rehab for the last several months doesn't mean we lost our touch!"

"Rehab? You've all be abusing your painkillers and the mini bars in your hotel rooms! All of you had plenty of time to rest and recuperate! If you spend it in a drug induced coma, that's your own damned faults! Reality never went anywhere! Time to deal with it. Also we need to help train the replacements for team Twelve."

Bryan bitterly asked, "So we're replaceable? Who's going to fill the shoes of Fred, Mindy and Nick?"

"Seems that out of all the Vanguard squadrons, we took the least amount of KIA's, killed in action. We're not getting replacements, so their boots will be vacant for some time."

Tara asked in shock, "How the hell are we so shorthanded that we can't get new personnel for our squad? We had a shit ton of cannon fodder to go around!" Lauren rolled her eyes as she lit up a cigar, "Why do I have to explain everything?"

"You're the only one that goes to the meetings and gets updates from the higher ups and our only source of information. Your program always this flaky, or did the decapitation do some permanent damage?" Jane snapped at her annoyed with seemingly everything. Lauren sighed, "Call me what you will. At least I haven't been killed. Like I said, we've taken the least amount of casualties. You saw how Olympus was. Multiply that. It's a miracle that most of us are here. Other Vanguard squads were completely wiped out. Almost every single new trainee, clone and android is going to fill those vacancies. Right now we and Twelve are the most experienced units left in the entire Vanguard. Plus, if I had to guess the next campaign, I would say it would be Earth itself."

"Why do you say that?" Bryan asked while lying face down. His back was still hurting. Lauren went on, "It's the most logical next target. When Earth falls, so does the Alliance. Yet unlike Mars and Jupiter, we're only getting a month to get ready for the next operation. We're literally going to be the first in this time, no cannon fodder units to be our shield, just us. Breathe easy, and enjoy the ride. We'll be meeting up with Twelve at Olympus soon."

Everyone sat back thinking about what they had just been told. Alec looked over to Duncan and Alisa seeing them both look depressed. Anyone would be after the injuries they suffered. Alec tapped Duncan's shoulder, "How are you holding up?"

Duncan only muttered some gibberish as he looked down quickly and started crying. Alisa leaned over to him, and both of them started weeping together. Alec backed off knowing he wouldn't completely understanding their loss. Bryan sighed, "Artificial organs just aren't the same."

Alec looked around with his new eyes. It seemed

similar to looking at a holographic screen. He nodded, "Yeah. Some things just aren't as good as the original. But isn't something better than nothing?"

"Beats being dead..." Jane shuddered after saying that and rubbed her head. The bus got quiet as it followed the highway up the mountain. It curved side to side as it went up, allowing the vehicle to travel at a low angle. The mountain brought back bad memories of that day. It looked almost untouched with all the dead bodies and equipment long since cleared off. The entire top of the mountain was covered in snow and ice. One of the cave entrances that was once sealed off was now open again. The bus stopped as a gate guard came in and checked everyone's identity. Once she was done, the bus was allowed into the mountain. The tunnel seemed to go on forever as everyone looked up at the lights that flashed by. There were other vehicles traveling around the tunnels going their own way along with personnel working on the equipment inside. There were still signs of the cave-ins with boulders and dirt still being removed. The bus finally came to a stop in front of a single steel door. The doors opened, and they all filed out. Lauren entered in a code and did an eye scan before the door opened. Once it did they had to go through an airlock before they were allowed to enter. Inside was a long passageway painted white that seemed to go on forever. Lauren led them along. It didn't take them long before they got to a classroom. Inside others were waiting for them. One of them stood up, "Dad?"

Duncan's eyes went wide and he seemed to have new life breathed into him. "Son?"

The two of them walked up to each other. They looked identical standing side by side. Duncan smiled, "It's been too long."

Duncan, Jr. started laughing, "Not long enough."

Suddenly Jr. punched Sr. in the face, knocking him down. Yeager stood up cheering, "That's right! Get back at your father!"

"So that's how it is?" Duncan, Sr. said as he got up wiping away the blood from his nose. Jr. said with his voice shaking, "Leave us will you?" He then tried to kick him in the groin. Sr. caught his kick with his legs, "Those are new, and I don't intend to lose them again. For what it's worth, I'm sorry I wasn't there. In all seriousness, calm down or I'll break your leg."

"You literally don't have the balls!" Duncan, Jr. snapped at him. He got slapped across the face twice so hard that marks were left behind. "I got new ones of those, too. Don't push it!" Sr. barked.

"Don't stop now! Keep hating your father!" Yeager

kept egging him on. Jane 68 went over to Jane 69 and asked, "Does everyone in your squad have daddy issues?"

"Don't get me started. How have you been?" Sixty nine asked 68. "Been killed twice… how about you?"

"Had every limb replaced at least once. Now if you want to have a pissing contest, I might lose the in the injuries department, but I know my teammates are a bigger pain in the ass than yours."

"Really? One got me killed because she's a shitty pilot." Sixty eight said looking over at Lauren. She sighed, "How was I to know the cockpit was that weak?"

"Two of mine never seem to stop about talking about how much their fathers suck. Also two of my dead teammates were in a love/hate relationship that got them killed." Sixty nine said. Sixty eight tried to come back, "Well we had a total psycho on our team that raped his inmates while in prison."

"The woman in the love/hate relationship used to put on a mask that was made of her own father's…" Sixty eight stopped her, "You win!"

"Great, a group crazier than us… we're doomed," Bryan sighed as he sat down with back pain so severe it made him cringe. Yeager went up to him and slapped him on the back, "No. The Alliance is doomed. We've killed a shit load of those assholes!"

Lauren went up to Kathryn, "Is that your…"

Kathryn nodded while smiling, "Yes. My son turned out okay, didn't he?"

"Yeah, one time I impaled a person on a shotgun, used it to prop him on the ground and then pulled the trigger! It was like a geyser going off with burning bones and shit flying in the air. The wound was so wide the shotgun went right through him. I was able to use it on another asshole!" Yeager said with great glee while Bryan looked at him and started to back away. Lauren looked at her with concern, "Well, he seems to be a product of his environment."

Alec came up to him, "I remember you just after you were conceived! You did grow up quick."

"She also said I grew quick," Yeager winked at him. Alec laughed, "Nice, how much did she get paid to say that?"

"I gave her a good tip," Yeager winked again. Mira sighed holding her head up, "This is going to go on a while, isn't it?"

"It did!" Yeager and Alec laughed. Lauren asked Kathryn, "You never answered the question on who the father was. Is it…?"

Kathryn looked surprised as she looked over at Alec and Yeager laughing. She shook her head side to side,

"No, it was an Alliance sailor. I know his last name was Marley, and he went by Cal. Think it might have been short for something. On the bright side, every time my baby shoots an Alliance soldier, he thinks it could be his father."

"That's completely normal," Lauren said looking at her with more concern. Alisa asked, "Are we going to get down to business or what?"

"Depends on what your business is," Yeager told her giving her a smile. Suddenly a voice shouted, "Attention on deck!"

Everyone stood up right as Victor walked in. He seemed to have more gray hair than before but not the white hair he had now. "At ease. Please take a seat," Victor told the teams.

Everyone sat down looking up at him. He smiled, "I'm proud. No, we are all proud of what you have done here."

There wasn't a single face in there that wasn't smiling at least somewhat. Victor went on, "You are all the toughest that the Corps has to offer. Both teams have been through their trials and came out the other side swinging. Not many others can say that. Don't worry. It won't be for nothing."

A holographic image of two massive arches that

were facing each other and almost completing a circle appeared in front of them. "This is the next operation," Victor informed them. "We're going to cut off the line of support to the Alliance freeing this system from Vegan control once and for all."

Everyone sat up in their seats looking at the station and anticipating what information was coming next. Victor told them, "Win this battle, and we win the war. No pressure except on our enemies. Any questions?"

"Can we crush their skulls with said pressure?" Yeager asked with glee in his eyes. Victor smiled, "You can do whatever you want to win. Each of you are going to earn your names as the Vanguard of the Sparta Corps this next mission! All of you must be ready for when the time comes. You won't have much time to train. Make the most of what time you have. I trust Kathryn and Lauren will fill you in on the details. Good luck, and good slaying."

"Attention!" was shouted again. Everyone stood up as they walked out the door. Once he was gone everyone sat down. Yeager moaned, "I was just getting used to this. I don't want the war to end."

"Then make it an ending you'll be proud of. It'll be fun," Alec nodded at him. The two of them seemed to get along really well. Lauren took the stage, "Okay. Let's get to work."

AWAKENING

CHAPTER 16
REVELATION
2222
SOL SYSTEM
PLUTO STATION
OBSERVATION DECK

ALEC was again sitting next to Yeager seemingly shooting the shit as they downed booze in a lounge. Alec acted as casually as he could this time just taking swigs of his drink. "Those were the days, huh Alec?"

Taking a wild guess, he replied, "Yeah. Good times."

"Yeah, remember when we got liberty out in Olympus City? That was a wild night," Yeager laughed thinking about it. Alec laughed too, "It's a little fuzzy. Could you remind me?"

"Be careful what you ask for. Some memories should be left forgotten," he told him as he took a swig. Alec egged him on, "Don't be a wuss. Tell me."

"You asked. So we were on liberty and the lot of us

are getting hammered, I mean really drunk. Hell even Victor showed up to party with us! We got drinks and food on the house! Spent a good two hours there drinking and eating. You and Tara went to the restroom to fuck, and everyone could hear you." Yeager started doing a good impersonation of Alec and Tara going back and forth between the two, "*It feels good! I always know how to please! Yes! That's right. Be positive for me! I was positive on my last test! What test?* There wasn't a silent person in that place. Everyone was laughing their asses off. You were freaking out! Turns out she was just messing with you. It was one hell of a joke! You tried getting her back by sleeping with Alisa. That backfired."

Alec was quietly giggling to himself, "Really how so?"

"You seem to be taking this lightly, same thing is going on. Both of you are going at it and start talking dirty. You said, *don't worry, I'm good!* She then told you, *not what she said!*"

Both of them started laughing in the lounge. It covered up the ambient noise of air filters humming. It took them a couple minutes to calm down. Yeager asked, "Why are you laughing? It was at your expense."

"I laugh at myself first before others, mama's boy," Alec winked at him. Yeager looked amused and mad at the same time, "Only you would call me that."

"What? Can't take a joke?" He wondered. Yeager told him, "That face! I know you just got control, but damn! I hate that face!" Alec started thinking about the reflection he saw earlier in the window. It seemed it was him. At the same time, it wasn't. Also he saw the same reflection in the last flashback. Yeager broke Alec's concentration when he threw his drink against the bulkhead. The plastic cup bounced around as Yeager sighed, "I thought it would shatter!"

"This is cheap shit after all..." Alec was feeling a bit woozy this time after all the drinking. He asked, "How are we getting drunk if we have artificial organs?"

"Doc gave us some pills to get drunk. Guess they're working!" Yeager laughed taking another drink. "He's only been this casual with me once before, and I've only seen him act this way with one other person," Alec thought to himself. He then plainly asked Yeager, "So you said something about my face? Did I always looked like this?"

Yeager laughed harder, "You're being a lightweight. We've only had four drinks, and you're already forgetting shit? That or that new body isn't as good as you thought it would be."

"New body? Who did it belong to again?" He asked Yeager while his eyes twitched slightly. He responded,

"You know that's my asshole father's body! I swear. If it wasn't for the fact that you're inside it, I would want to punch that face in! We've always been cool Al. You said you're going to change it anyway, right?"

Marley's drink slipped out of his hands, and his face went pale. He thought about everything, and it all started to add up: why Yeager called him dad, why Doc and Yosemite were being so cryptic, why Yeager hated him so much, why he was losing control. Marley uttered, "Son of a bitch."

"What was that?" Yeager started to lean back in his seat as he put his cup down. When they made eye contact Marley told him, "Son of a bitch!"

Marley flipped the table into Yeager's face knocking him backwards on the deck. Marley went down, grabbed him by the throat and lifted him up. Yeager gasped, "Is that any way to treat your son?"

"So I'm not Alec Dumont? Guess my last name is Marley. What's the first?" He asked releasing just a little bit of pressure on his throat. Yeager smiled, "Calvin, Calvin Marley. Now that you know enough of the truth…"

Yeager kicked him in the chest. Marley went back falling on the deck. He rolled over missing a kick. Marley rolled back the opposite way punching Yeager in the face. Before he could recover, Marley again grabbed him by the throat, lifted him up and slammed him against another table, smashing it. Marley was suddenly kicked in the gut and sent flying upside down into a vending machine. Both Yeager and Marley got up at the same time, He asked, "Besides being your father, what did I do to piss you off so bad?"

Yeager threw a part of the table at him; he ducked down missing it. Yeager closed the distance and caught Marley with a punch to the face, "You weren't there…!"

Another punch went across Marley's face, "… you used my mother as a whore…!"

Another punch hit him, "…and you're part of the Alliance!"

He swung again. Marley ducked down missing it. He came up with a punch to his side and elbowed Yeager in the face. When he faced away from him, Marley kicked him in the back, sending him crashing into another table. He didn't wait for Yeager to recover. He looked for the nearest exit and started running. So many thoughts were running through his head when he ran right into Kathryn. She knocked Marley down with a single punch flat on his back. He felt like the wind had been knocked out of him. She crouched down next to Marley as he looked up at her and laughed, "So I was the nerd that knocked you up? That doesn't mean we can't get along right?"

She grew an evil smiled and kicked him in the gut, "Use me as a fuck doll will you!"

She kicked him again. Marley laughed, "Is it weird that I'm getting aroused right now?"

Again she kicked. This time he rolled out of the way, tripping her over and kicking her in the face. Yeager ran over, "Don't you touch my mother!"

"I already did. That's how you got here!" Marley picked Kathryn up and threw her into Yeager knocking them both down at the same time. He turned around and ran away from them. He made a mad dash, flying thought the passageways because of the low gravity environment. Marley felt woozy and sick at the same time. He wondered what else was in that drink and where he should go. He needed some armor. Marley tried to access the base's maps, but nothing came up in his eyes. Running blind, he ran into Cullen and Mira. The two of them seemed to be waiting for him with stun sticks. Cullen asked Marley, "Where do you think you're going?"

"To give Cullen's mother some physical pleasure that dad can't give any more. You can have the sloppy seconds," Marley said cracking a smile. He never knew he could be such a smartass under pressure. The two them started circling him waving around the electrified metal rods. Mira told him, "Sorry, Alec won't like that."

"I'm not that asshole," Marley said as he took a glance at the two of them, seeing who would try to stick first. Cullen laughed, "Things change."

Cullen lunged first. Marley stepped out of the way causing him to shock Mira instead. She went down like a brick. Marley took advantage of the confusion and elbowed Cullen in the head over and over again. He grabbed the stick out of Cullen's hand, but lost hold of it. Both of them went for their side arm. Marley was able to grab it out of his holster and shove it under Cullen's chin and pull the trigger. Mira screamed as she pulled her side arm. Marley quickly shot her in between the eyes, "Some things stay the same!"

Marley kept going down the passageway. He saw the locker room where the armored suits where stored and pushed ahead. Marley suddenly saw Alec standing in front of him. "Do you really think you can get away?" asked Alec.

"What the fuck?" Marley said in shock. The real Alec smiled as he walked up to his doppelganger, "Where there's a will, there's always a way."

Alec walked towards Marley as he fired his pistol over and over again. Once he ran out of ammo, he saw none of his rounds hit. Alec then swung his fist at Marley's face. He tried to block it, but he couldn't move his limbs.

Marley got hit in the nose, yanking his head backwards. He took another punch to the face, making him stumble. Marley looked up at a glass window and saw he was punching himself. He looked again and saw Alec kicking him in the chest. Marley went backwards into a swarm of others. They stood around with armored suits soon joined by Kathryn and Yeager. Alec told them, "Don't worry. I've got this."

The others stared in awe as Marley literally bet himself up. Alec grabbed him by the throat and lifted him up, "Just slip away like you're supposed to! This is my body now! I stole it fair and square!"

One thing Marley noticed was that Alec only used the right side of his body. He looked around to see Jane looking over at him. They stared at each other for the longest second. She lifted up her pistol, aimed at Marley with a loose grip and winked one of her eyes. He reached back, pulled the pistol out of her hands and shot his own right hand off. Both Alec and Marley cried in pain at the same time. The others gasped in shock by the act. He recovered and put the hot pistol muzzle to his own throat, "Don't move or I'll shot!"

Some of them started laughing, "Really?"

Alec cried, "You assholes! I'm in danger! Back off!"

More people started laughing. Marley looked in

the mirror and started laughing at the image of himself taking his own body hostage. Alec snapped, "Stop laughing! I don't want to die... again!"

As everyone laughed Marley walked backwards into the locker room. "Wait you idiots! He's moving away!" screamed Alec.

Marley closed the door to the locker room and shot the controls buying him some time. He went over to his locker and donned his suit. It came out in an open shell, and he stepped back inside of it. It wrapped around him in seconds. Once it was on, he went over to the armory in the same area and grabbed a plasma shotgun and a couple grenades. The door was soon busted open as the operatives rushed in. Alec cried, "Save me idiots!"

Marley rushed forward opening fire. The first blast sounded like thunder as it went off. Bright pellets flew through the air, impacting into three people. Their shields burst like a bubble. The second shot burned their armor, and the third went right through them. He lobbed a grenade out the door causing the others to back off. Right after it went off, widening the exit, Marley rushed out making a mad dash for the nearest hanger bay. He followed his head up display as it pointed him in the right direction. Marley didn't pay any attention to who was following him or who was ahead. He blindly fired backwards as he went along.

Marley moved his artificial legs as fast as he could. It didn't take long before he got to the hanger. He went for the first craft he saw: a Hawk fighter. He hopped into the cockpit and activated the fighter. The holographic images showed Marley a full three sixty degree view of the area around him. Thankfully, controls were similar to that of the Crain. The restraints ripped from the fighter as he moved it forward. Marley fired away at the door in front of him with it turning red hot after a hundred plasma rounds. He pushed the fighter to full speed and crashed through the door. Marley jetted off into space and away from Pluto as fast as the Hawk could go. Surprisingly, there weren't any shots fired at the craft, nor were there any other fighters chasing after him. As Pluto got smaller and smaller, Alec asked, "Why the hell aren't they coming after me?"

"You're not worth it apparently!" Marley told him as he set the autopilot for the nearest Alliance outpost. Alec huffed, "Why do you think we got away so easily? Don't you think it's a bit odd?"

"Besides finding out I've been lied to, everyone that I sort of know is now trying to kill me, you are trying to steal my body, and I had to shoot my own hand to save myself. No, nothing else really seems that odd to me anymore!"

"Try? I think it's working so far," Marley's right hand and leg started moving involuntarily. He started tapping the controls. Alec commented, "You're going to knock yourself out?"

"I don't want to have to deal with you!" He kept tapping away at the holo-controls as alarms started to go off. Alec sighed, "You're just being petty now. Once you get to know me, I'm not that bad."

"You're trying to steal my body! I was born with it! It's mine!" Marley snapped at him as more alarms went off. Alec asked, "Have you had any real dreams?"

"I've only been seeing your past," he answered him as the fighter started slowing down. Alec smiled, "You thought it was your own, didn't you?"

Another alarm went off as Marley tapped the controls. Alec told him, "Well, you're in for a treat when the past catches up with you."

The fighter jumped speed and Marley's head flew backwards into the chair. Everything went black.

CHAPTER 17
2212
ASSAULT
SOL SYSTEM
CRAIN TRANSPORT
CARGO HOLD

EVERYONE seemed overly quiet as they waited inside the transport. They sat in their seats with the harnesses holding them in. All the lights were shut off leaving them in the dark. The transports were covered in rocks to make them look like asteroids to hide their approach. They'd been waiting for what felt like days. Alec tried breaking the silence, "So Duncan, how's your son?"

"We actually managed to reconcile... slightly," he told him with a hint of optimism in his voice. Alec went on, "Now, how did that come about? He tried to kill you."

Duncan laughed, "Yeah. We just talked after we beat each other one day, and I found out that most of his rage is borrowed from Yeager. So now at least we're communicating. At least now I have new reason to go on.

I want to try to reconnect with him."

"That's good. Yeager might be angry, but he's not a bad person once you get to know him," Alec said. Bryan started laughing, "Isn't he the one that put the microphone in the head letting us listen to you while Alisa and Tara questioned your performance?"

"I got him back when I dirty dicked his drink!" Alec laughed, the others started laughing harder. "What?"

"He didn't fall for that shit! He switched his drink with Lauren." Bryan told him. Lauren snapped, "What?"

Everyone in the compartment was now laughing. Lauren was staring at Alec with her hands balled up into fists. Alec shook his head, "Guess I've found a new reason to survive, getting him back."

"Be careful. Lauren might beat you to the punch." Jane told him. Lauren grumbled, "If he wasn't technically my nephew, I would kill him."

"I think he thought you were Kathryn. Why would he want her to have a tainted drink?" Alisa asked. Lauren shook her head, "If I make it through this, I'm going to cut that damned umbilical cord between them."

"Like I said, I got my son away from Yeager, and we get along." Duncan told everyone. Alec said, "Okay, enough about that literal and metaphorical freak child. What are we going to do when this is over?"

There was a long pause as everyone thought about it. At one point there was only the sound of the engines humming. Lauren put it bluntly, "We need to make it through this last mission first if any of us are going to think about retirement."

After she said that reality set in as the red lights came on. The harnesses automatically came off allowing them to float freely in the compartment. There was a series of sighs knowing what was about to come. Duncan joked to ease tensions, "Look Bryan! Back in the red light district!"

"That's nice. You can get laid for once," Bryan told him. Lauren snapped, "Enough! We can mess around later. Focus on the here and now. We've been hammering this for months! Pay attention at once." She pulled up the images of two crescent shaped stations that were side by side. The one on the left got enlarged. Two dots popped up with thirteen on the bottom section and twelve on the top. Tara asked, "Do we really have to go over this again?"

"Did we not harp enough that this operation is fucking important? We're going over this one last time while we can." She pointed to the lower section, "Both our teams are going in at the same time from different sections. We need to be quiet and quick. Team Twelve and their support units are going to act as decoys while we go in with the bombs. They'll hold them off and keep them distracted while we destabilize the station's reactors. There's also the secondary objective: data mine the computers on the station for info. I don't know why, but they seem to care about that a little more. So two birds, one stone as the ancients would say. Another thing making it harder for us is that we're going out against Alliance operatives that have equipment that's on par with our own. They have armored suits, more powerful partial weapons and energy shielding. We do have one advantage. Our suits have been installed with an experimental cloaking device that will make us invisible unless we make major movements or fire. Remember, fast is slow. Slow is steady. Any questions?"

No one said anything. Jane said it best, "Let's kill them and leave." Lauren smiled, "Time to make a difference. Get ready."

The transport rocked as it landed on the surface of the station. Everyone went against the bulkhead from the motion. They pushed themselves back into position as the bottom door open up showing a smooth gray hull with a burn mark in the center. It made the metal thin enough so it could be cut though. Lauren reached over to Alec tapping his shoulder, "We got this."

He didn't know if she was trying to convince herself or the squad. Everyone just nodded to get their confidence up. Duncan and Tara went down first to the hull and cut through the metal with blow torches. This gave them access inside the station. One by one they leaped down inside. They ended up in a small cramped tube that ran near the exterior of the station. Tara took point leading the rest of them though the cramped spaces. It was surrounded with pipes and cords wrapped together. Surprisingly, for being seven feet tall and having armored suits with gear attached, they managed to squeeze their way through the tight spaces. They came upon the overhead to a passageway. Tara cut a hole wide enough for her to fit through. She held still as her cloak activated. If it wasn't for the marker on their head up display, they wouldn't know she was there. She came over the communication link, "Clear."

Next Duncan leaped down with his cloak activating. Both of them went against the bulkhead as a set of soldiers walked past them. Both of them wore armored suits similar to theirs except their helmets had human faces instead of skulls. They went by without noticing either one of them. Lauren and Bryan went down next forming up along the bulkhead. Alisa and Jane went down next. Everyone spread out as far as they could. Two operatives walked by in their armored suits. They looked almost identical to the Iron Clad armor save the masks that looked like human faces. The two of them passed right by them and didn't even see them. Alec was the last one to leap down. Once he landed he was right in front of a crowd of people. He waited in the center of the passageway slowly backing up with the others. They climbed up the passageway using their feet and legs to prop themselves in position.

Alec went into the crowd moving his way from person to person without touching them and moving himself out of their way. Once he was on the other side of the crowd, one operative stayed behind looking back. He started walking towards Alec as he stood frozen in his place hoping he wouldn't be seen. The soldier lost focus as alarms went off. He went the opposite direction leaving them alone. The others dropped down from the ceiling. Lauren sighed, "That was close. Follow me."

She took point leading the others behind her. They kept a single file line as they went ahead. They heard a set of footsteps from behind them. The team ducked into a doorway and out of the way as they would pass by. Being more cautious they went from door to door as they moved along. The passageway seemed to curve as they went on. The team kept their movements limited, not wanting to draw attention from the security systems. None of them said anything as they went along. They managed to keep their breathing to a minimum as they moved forward. Every couple of minutes they would have to move out of the way of more Alliance personnel moving though the passageway.

Finally the team came upon a ladder well. One by one they went in, climbing up the decks as fast as they could. Lauren signaled them to stop as the waited for a group of Alliance operatives to clear out. Once they did, Lauren signaled for the rest of them to move. She walked faster as they got closer to the core section of the station. They came upon the large doors that led into the compartment. The team stacked up on both sides of the door waiting to breach. All of them prepped their weapons while keeping them pointed away from one another.

Lauren opened the door exposing the massive core above them. It looked like a huge horizontal cylinder with lightning being streamed inside. The area was mostly vacant except for a couple of guards. They were walking around roving the area. Each person found a target to stalk, following them around the compartment. The bulkheads were covered in holographic controls along with images of the statuses of the station's systems. The orange seemed to even out the massive amount of blue light emanating from the core. As the team members got closer to their targets, Lauren signaled them to take them out. Duncan went up and snapped the neck of his target. Alisa stabbed hers. Tara shot the person in front of her in the head. Bryan bashed the skull of the engineer in front of him. Jane shot her victim. Lauren stabbed hers, and Alec also bashed the head of his target. "Clear!"

"All clear!" echoed in the empty room. They dropped their cloaks, confident they weren't needed. Duncan and Alisa went over to the nearest computer and started hacking. Tara and Bryan started planting the bomb. Alec, Jane and Lauren breathed a sigh of relief. Lauren shouted, "Half way there!"

"As much as I want to say that was easy, I don't like to get ahead of myself," Alec said as he took a couple breaths. He went over to Tara, "Hey. When we get out of here, I want to get you a drink."

"That's nice. You be happy to know I took more joy out of you getting embarrassed than being hurt by you trying to sleep around." She looked up at him. He laughed, "I figured next time would be more private. I would love to spend more time getting to know you better."

"Crappy pick up line, but I'll meet you half way. Who knows? We might have sex out of passion instead of to ease nerves this time," she told him as she helped Bryan place the round bomb into place. Alec nodded, "I would like that."

Duncan shouted, "Get over here! I think you all want to see this!"

"All done," Bryan said as the squad formed up on the monitor Bryan was working on. Lauren asked, "What did you find?"

"A lot. Too much. As the ancients would say, this is too good to be true. Maybe this explains how we got in here so easily," he said as he tapped away on the holo-controls showing images of Vegan operatives and a Stallion operative, too. He went on, "This can't be right. Everything here seems set up. I'm digging a little deeper."

He tapped away on the controls as Alisa suddenly yelled frantically, "Disconnect the bomb!"

"What?" Everyone asked at the same time. Alisa snapped as she stood up grabbing Bryan, "Disconnect it!"

"Why?" Jane asked her, confused as everyone else was. Duncan snapped, "Too late!"

Suddenly the core flashed brightly blinding all of them. The whole compartment was filled with a loud clap deafening them. They held their helmets as they stumbled around. Lauren quickly snapped, "What the fuck?"

"We didn't plant a bomb! We planted an electromagnetic pulse device!" Bryan shouted with fear in his voice. Lauren asked, "Can you deactivate it?"

"After all the trouble we put into it so it couldn't be

deactivated? We'll try." Bryan and Tara went to work trying to remove the device as Jane asked, "Why the hell is the bomb acting like an EMP device?"

"I don't know! This doesn't add up! We got this damned thing from Yosemite himself! It was part of something to do with Icarus! That asshole must have screwed us!" Lauren was starting to panic. She went over to Alisa, "Anything else we need to know?"

"The names and targets on this list weren't our objective! These coordinates are in different parts of the galaxy," She told them showing them the list. Alec looked down at it seeing every person's name and location, "What?"

Duncan got up, "I think we've been had!"

"No shit! When does our fleet show up?" Jane asked. Lauren sighed, "Five minutes…"

Bryan panicked as he said, "If this goes off, they'd be in range of the blast. They'd be sitting ducks!"

"Do whatever it takes to stop that from happening!" Lauren told them. Both Tara and Bryan frantically worked away on the device. Lauren instructed, "Take position in front of the exits. I have the feeling we'll have company soon enough. If we can't get the device deactivated in time, shut down your suits and equipment."

"Why?" Alec asked her. She explained, "If we have

our equipment on when that damned thing go off, we're screwed! Cover the entrances!"

Everyone not working on the bomb took cover where they could. Jane snapped, "This is bullshit!"

"Couldn't agree more! Why would the higher ups care more about a fucking list then winning?" Alec asked. Lauren asked, "How's it coming?"

"Don't fucking interrupt! If it goes off, you'll know how it's coming!" Tara shouted at her. Lauren went on the communications link, "Kathryn! Get your team out!"

Suddenly there was an even brighter flash than before. Everyone covered their masks as the light only got brighter. Everyone shut down their suits as they fell flat on the deck. It seemed like storm came in as lightning bolts shot into anything electronic. The lights started fading out and the gravity went off. Everyone floated up into the air with the bolts flying past them. Each one of them suddenly got struck by the lightning sending them back down to the floor. Alec was the last one to get hit as everything went black for him.

CHAPTER 18
2222
REUNION
SOL SYSTEM
UNKNOWN LOCATION

MARLEY saw a Vegan in front of him getting punched in the head over and over again. There was green blood coming out of his eyes, nose holes and mouth. He let go, letting the dead alien lay down on the deck. There were several others laying around dead with blast marks all over the bulkheads. Marley was inside what looked like a hanger bay and the Hawk fighter he'd come in was crashed against one of the bulkheads with several Alliance operatives pinned in between. Above were several blasted out auto turrets with sparks flying out of them. Alarms were going off and red lights were flashing. "Alec?" he asked.

"Still here," Alec responded. Marley looked around at the carnage as he heard footsteps coming and ducked behind the crashed Hawk fighter. "What the fuck is going on? What did you make me do?" Marley whispered loudly.

"Don't recognize the place yet? Well as for the amphibian, he told me something I didn't like, so I killed him and his friends. The other cronies aren't too happy with you now," he told him with glee in his voice. The Alliance operatives came into the hanger bay with their weapons at the ready looking around for signs of life. They checked the dead bodies and looked underneath shards of debris. Marley was about to stand up when Alec stopped him, "They'll kill you if you do that. You're their enemy now."

"You made me a traitor?" He snapped at him quietly. Alec laughed, "You pretended to be me, and I thought it would be fair to pretend to be you. Turns out they were going to kill you anyway. Like I said, they thought you were a traitor! Besides you want freedom as much as any of us do."

"Freedom? I've been a fucking patsy this whole time! How's that liberating?" He asked as the operatives got closer to him. Marley reached down and grabbed an assault rifle and checked to see how much ammo it had. Alec told him, "We got fucked over. I want to find out who screwed us. We'll get confirmation on who screwed us."

"Confirmation? It was Yosemite. Wasn't it?"

Marley asked him as the operatives were almost on top of them. Alec explained, "Regardless, we're in this together like it or not. These people are fucked with or without our help. So either you can fight them or you can die. Up to you."

He thought about it, "But, I was on their side! I might know these people!"

"Sorry, but I got to twist your arm," Alec told him. He lobbed a grenade over the top of the fighter right into the center of a group of soldiers. It exploded before it hit the ground. The blast almost ripped them in two. Alec used Marley's right arm to reach down and grab another rifle. "Isn't duel wielding a bad idea?" Marley asked.

"Yes, but it looks bad ass," Alec explained. Marley went around the corner controlling the left arm and Alec controlling the right. Both of them fired at the same time. They took turns firing. The triggers were pulled with rapid succession driving off the operatives. They ducked down to have their shield recharge. Alec threw another grenade at a group of them and it exploded right above them. "Too late to turn back now!" Alec smiled.

Marley felt his right arm reach over for the pistol and pull it out. His right leg made a stretch forward and he moved his left to start a run. Alec forced Marley to head for the exit as the operatives recovered from the last volley.

Both of them moved their limbs so they were able to run. The door in front of them started closing. They both shoved the legs down on the ground and leaped through just as the two doors slammed shut. Marley planted a grenade on the door in case anyone wanted to follow. He asked, "How did we get on this Alliance station?"

"Like I said, I pretended to be you, made a good sob story on how I got tricked and was being used. Just like you really were." Alec told him. They went down the passageway and it look oddly familiar. "You'd think they would have just shot us down," said Marley.

"I lied and told them I had intel for them. I do that a lot," Alec laughed. Marley tapped on a backpack and asked, "What's in there?"

"Same thing that screwed us over the last time, just more of it." Alec pulled them into a door way as more soldiers came charging after them. Marley placed a grenade right in their path. The footsteps came to a sudden halt when they ran right over it. The blast shook the passageway as smoke and metal shards went in the air. Marley came out the doorway and walked over the dead. Alec shot them twice to make sure they stayed that way. As they passed by cross sections, Marley would check left and Alec would check the right. Marley wondered, "Why do you think it would be a good idea to use it twice? Also, wouldn't they have changed their systems to stop it from happening again?"

"The trap isn't for us this time. Also they didn't bother to change the systems at all. Victory will soon defeat them," Alec said as they reached the same ladder well as before. Both of them climbed up while seeing flashes of the past. They kept climbing until they reached the main deck. There were several operatives waiting for them. Marley tossed a grenade up through the door. They didn't have time to react. The blast forced the doors open with fire and smoke coming into the ladder well. Alec reached up and aimed his pistol around the corner checking for any survivors. A couple shots rang out. "Clear."

Marley went up onto the deck checking both passageways for personnel. Three auto turrets suddenly came down from the overhead aiming at them. He quickly rolled back into the ladder well as the shots rang out. The bulkheads around the entrance quickly grew red hot with the rounds impacting into it. Marley looked down seeing he only had one grenade left. "I have an idea. Just roll with it," Marley told Alec.

Marley leaped up back onto the deck and tossed the grenade to his left impacting into one of the turrets. It ripped from the overhead crashing into the deck with sparks flying everywhere. Marley rolled forward as the auto turret in front of him fired away missing every shot. He got right up underneath it, jumped up, grabbed the weapon and ripped it off of its mount. Marley back over to the last turret and used the machinegun to destroy it. "It's clear now," he said.

Marley walked into the core chamber seeing it looked almost the same as it did before. The same holographic panels and the same cylinders hung above with the lightning. Marley went over to the same area that the bomb was placed before. He pulled the heavy object off of his back and placed it near the core and connected it. "Wait, how did a fighter that just left Pluto get across the system to here so fast?"

"We had some help in that area. Our friends from Pluto gave us a boost. Really thought we got away from them so easily?" Alec said after the device was attached. "They're helping us with this? What's really going on?" asked Marley.

"A second chance. Meanwhile..." Marley lost control of his body for a second as Alec switched on the device. It hummed as the lightning in the tube started flashing rapidly. "...We're going to have some time and possibly some people to kill soon enough. Meanwhile you and I both want some answers; don't we?"

"Remember the saying about being careful what

you ask for? Also, why would anyone on Pluto help us get here?" Marley asked him as he started hacking into the database of the station. Alec hummed as he went through the records and files, "Don't know. He was being all mysterious and shit."

"Mysterious? Sounds like Doc. Also, Yosemite is so the one that threw you assholes under the bus! Just because you didn't like hearing it from a frog doesn't make it less true!" Marley guessed as Alec snapped, "He was being an asshole. Why did you think I was smashing his fucking skull in?"

He focused on one file in particular. Alec opened it and examined it carefully. It played a video file over and over. It was just two Vegans talking to each other. Something must have caught his eye. For all Marley knew this could have been what the ancients called a wild goose chase. Alec focused on the conversation. It was between two Vegans and the dialect sounded like frogs crocking. The program he was using seemed to be able to translate the language into something more understandable. The two aliens were talking about a plan they had concocted. Marley was still trying to work it out when Alec uttered, "Son of a bitch!"

"Are you talking about Yeager or his mother?" Marley asked sarcastically. Alec laughed, "One of the frogs is being a deadbeat to the other and not paying up on a bet. What a jerk, right?"

"A bet? That's what's got your interest?" Marley asked rolling his eyes in dismay.

"You should be interested, too. They're sending people in to kill us right now." Suddenly the doors came open with grenades flung in by the dozen. They ducked down behind a computer console as the grenades went off. It felt like they were surrounded by fireworks. The deck vibrated violently going up and down. Shards of shrapnel flew in the air piercing everything. The console stood up to the abuse of the shrapnel cutting into it. Alec snapped, "There's always people trying to kill me because of you assholes!"

"Fuck you! It's not your ass on the line right now!" Marley snapped at him. He peeked around the corner with Alec aiming the machinegun. Four operatives came charging in. Alec quickly shot them down in a hail of partial fire. The weapon had one heavy recoil as it almost knocked them down. More grenades flew in and they again ducked for cover. As the grenades went off, Marley yelled, "You keeping talking about freedom! That's bullshit! Those machines and clones were dragged into this just like you were!"

"At least it's equal! Everyone is disposable to our

leaders, organic and artificial! Got to love equality!" Alec told him in an overly cheery way. The operatives walked forward side by side combining the strength of their shields. Alec fired away, but each shot was absorbed. "Any grenades left?" Alec inquired.

"No. Can't you do the overload thing with that machinegun?" Marley asked as they got closer. Right in front of him the bulkhead exploded sending a solid piece flying forward slamming on the deck. "Give me a minute."

Alec used Marley's right arm to quickly manipulate the machinegun while Marley used his rifle. He waited and fired when a grenade flew in. When the round impacted into the grenade the explosion gave them enough time to get away from the operatives. They leaped over another console as the machinegun started overheating. Quickly, they tossed it away and it exploded right in the center of the operatives, ripping their legs off. Marley ran forward into the breach as more soldiers came in for them. He swung the rifle like a club, hitting one of them in the head and kicking him forward into his friends as they came in behind them.

Alec grabbed another rifle, and when the operatives got clustered together both Alec and Marley shot them over and over again. Several of them went down in the fury of fire. Alec ran out of ammo for his weapon.

He reached down to one of the dead and pulled her up. Marley saw grenades attached to her hips and activated one of them. Alec threw her across the room into a group of soldiers. The blast cut them in half as they ran forward. Marley looked back to the breach seeing a rifle get pointed in. He shot the hands holding it. The person leaned forward screaming and Marley shot him again in the head. That used up his last round for the rifle. He went through the breach and muscle struck an operative in the stomach.

Alec reached down pulling the pistol from his holster and shot him in the head. Marley shoved forward on the dead body and pushed him into one of his partners. Alec pointed the pistol behind them and shot another soldier in the head. Marley went back grabbing another pistol and the two of them fired one by one at the operatives in front of them. Marley ducked behind a wounded soldier and used her as a shield. He moved forward kneeing her in the head hard enough that her neck snapped loudly. Marley stuck his pistol muzzle into the face of another operative and blasted part of his head off. Alec reached over and got another headshot. Marley went to the side knocking the rifle barrel with his legs and shot the person in the neck. Alec got two more kills before running out of ammo. He then threw the pistol so hard it impaled someone in the head. Marley ran out of ammo and ditched the pistol. He reached down for a rifle and yanked one out of the dead hands of a soldier. He went around the next corner swing the muzzle into the first face mask he saw with enough force that the soldier's neck snapped.

Marley saw his rifle had a grenade launcher underneath the main barrel. He pulled the trigger, and the explosive round knocked one operative into the others. Once they were clustered together, the round exploded taking them all out. The ground was covered in so much blood that it was hard not to slip in it. Marley grabbed a couple more ammo packs and a pistol in the hull. He started getting alarms from his suit, indicating he'd taken a lot of damage while in the fight. Parts of his armor fell off as he went back to the core room seeing the process was almost done. Marley had to remove his face mask because it was too badly dented in to see out of. Alec was pulling shrapnel shards from their shared body as Marley asked, "When does this damned thing go off?"

"Soon," Alec told him. A voice behind him barked, "Are you talking to yourself?"

Marley looked behind him seeing a woman. She removed her face mask. He didn't know exactly why, but her face looked familiar. Her dark skin, those round eyes, the black hair, small chin and thin lips. She looked at him with rage while holding her side trying to keep herself from bleeding out. "What of it? No one else wanted a conversation."

"Marley? Calvin? Is that really you?" She snapped at him aiming a partial shotgun. "Mostly. Who are you?" he retorted.

"Really? It's Benson... what do you mean by mostly? As opposed to what? Hardly?" She snapped at him getting closer. Alec asked, "What is it with you and crazy women?"

"Wait. How did you just speak in a different voice?" She asked as she came forward. Marley lowered his rifle as she asked, "So you did turn on us! No wonder the brass didn't trust you! I stuck up for you, and this is how your repay me, how you repay all the operators that you worked with and just killed? Why?"

"Why was I abandoned?"

"You were declared dead!"

"I got better," both Marley and Alec said at the same time. It was odd to hear two voiced speak with only one mouth. She barked, "What the fuck did they do to you? You're working for them now? You've always been overly sensitive, but really, you couldn't take a couple jokes or criticism? You said you couldn't be rewritten!"

"It's a long story. To make it short..." Marley tried

to tell her. She yelled, "Every time someone says that, it's not short!"

Marley laughed, "Oh come on! I'm not going to give you my life story. I don't even remember anything! I didn't even know who I really was until recently," he explained to her. She shook her head, "Why the hell are you still working with them then? Why are you doing this? Because you're programmed?"

"There's another personality in my head. He forced my hand," he told her. Alec oddly backed him up, "It's true. We've been kind of using him."

"You've lost it! I should have known better! Wait, what did you do to the core?" She asked as the reactor above started doing the same thing it did earlier all over again. This time it was more violent. Alec snapped, "Same thing you assholes did to the Sparta Corps years ago! Karma's going to have her day!"

"You idiots. You've killed us all! You're not setting off an EMP!" They could hear fear in her voice as the room started glowing red. Both Alec and Marley asked, "What?"

There was a sudden flash blinding everyone. Everything felt hot as a high pitched scream went through the air. When things cleared up Benson was down on her knees with her shotgun in her hands. She looked up at Marley with burned skin and tears coming out of her eyes,

"Who's the puppet master this time?"

There was another flash but no screaming this time. Marley walked forward with his vision clearing again. This time Benson was flat on the deck and still as a rock. All that was left of her head was charred flesh and bones. He asked Alec, "What did we just do?"

Alec's voice trembled, "I don't know."

They heard the thundering sound of metal boots stampeding towards them. The operatives charged into the room about the fire when the core flashed once more. Everyone was blinded, and the sound of screaming filled their ears.

CHAPTER 19
HUNTED
2212
SOL SYSTEM
ALLIANCE SLIP GATE STATION
MAIN CORE ROOM

EVERYONE quickly came to as their suits reactivated. The room was pitch black with no lights at all inside the station. The team activated night vision looking at the blank walls and the seemingly empty cylinder. They took up positions around the room guarding the exits. Lauren asked while holding back her rage, "Who's up?"

Everyone spook up as they checked their equipment. Thankfully they were able to turn almost everything off before the EMP surge was activated. Bryan uttered, "We fucked up…"

"We got set up! Let's get out of here while we still can. Someone has to make that bastard pay!" Lauren said. In the quiet of the station they heard a couple sets of footsteps running around. It multiplied echoing in the area. Lauren ordered, "We make for the hanger bay. We'll jack one of the Alliance transports and run to some place friendly. I'll take point."

Alisa pointed out, "Our fucking cloaking devices didn't survive the pulse! How are we going to get there without being seen?"

Lauren snapped, "We kill any bastards that get in the way! Don't be a wuss, and let's go already!" She went up to one of the doors and quickly forced it open. Duncan quickly peeked around the corner and signaled the others to follow. Lauren went out first checking one part of the passageway and Duncan came out covering her. The others followed being extremely cautious as they kept their weapons up at the ready. They kept hearing footsteps both ahead and behind them. Lauren looked back at them, "Relax. There's only two directions they could come from."

Suddenly a blast door closed cutting her off from the rest of the team. There was a wide port hole where the others could see her. Bryan and Alec went for the door trying to lift it up. Lauren was suddenly attacked by two Alliance soldiers. They both had on the new armored suits and used heavy weapons. The two round they shot instantly heated up the door making Alec and Bryan back off. Duncan snapped, "Stand back!"

He took a couple of shots at the door only getting

a couple red spots. Alisa snapped, "We have light weapons! They can't blast though that!"

Lauren had leaped up dodging the first rounds and fired back at them. They stumbled backwards as their shield flashed after every hit. They ducked behind a corner blindly firing back at her. She leaped back down firing at the corner to keep them pinned. Lauren kicked with her back leg as hard as she could causing small dents. Tara asked, "Anyone got any explosives?"

They quickly gathered every grenade they had as the Alliance operatives threw their own grenade at Lauren. She leaped forward and went around the corner as the grenade went off taking cover. The transparent metal cracked from the force. Lauren came right around again and got right up close to one of the soldiers and rammed her weapon up underneath the jaw of the person. She pulled the trigger over and over. The person's head yanked back after every shot. It took five times for the round to go all the way though the persons head and out their helmet. The other operative got a clear shot while Lauren shoved the dying operative forward as a shield. She took a partial round in the torso sending her backwards while the dead soldier fell face first to the ground. Lauren and the other operative fired at each other at the same time hitting each other over and over again. Lauren shot the weapon out of his hand just as she ran out of ammo. She threw it at him and gave him an upper cut. Alisa started placing the grenades on the door as shots suddenly came over their heads. Other operatives were taking pot shots at them. Alec, Duncan and Bryan went back firing rounds to fend them off. Jane commented, "They're toying with us."

"I'll show them what comes of using us as their playthings without paying first," Bryan lobbed his only grenade down the passageway. The punch forced the Alliance operatives backwards as he pulled out his side arm. Lauren was hit in the head and sent against the bulkhead with her helmet cracking. The operative charged forward and swung his pistol at her. She ducked down missing the punch. She ripped off her helmet and used it to hit his chin lifting his head right up. Lauren then stabbed him in the throat with a plasma knife. Alisa shouted, "Fire in the hole!"

The door was ripped open as it tore in two. Lauren ducked down missing the shards as they flew over her. As it slammed on the deck she turned around smiling, "Took you all long enough. Out fucking stand..."

A round entered though the back of her head and came out her face. There was blood, sparks and metal flying forward onto the rest of the squad as they stood there in shock. Jane went forward grabbing Lauren's dead body as it fell forward. Two operative went backwards out of sight while the others fired at him. Tara screamed, "Bastard!"

"No!" Jane cried as she held her. Her face was completely gone with only a wide burnt hole in its place. Bryan asked, "She can come back right? Right?"

"We need to make it to find out," Alec went forward, "Can't do that standing around here! Let's go!"

"Who put you in charge?" Alisa asked. He told her, "That asshole who killed Lauren. Let's fucking go!"

The others either didn't care enough or were too shocked to argue. Jane quickly laid down Lauren's body as she joined the others going down the passageway. Alec took one last look as he moved on. As much as Alec wanted to follow the person that took out their leader, he knew they had to escape. They came upon an elevator that was out of order. Duncan and Bryan forced it open. It looked like a long empty shaft going down as far as their eyes could see. Bryan laughed, "You're stupid for bringing this rope they said. We won't need it they said."

"Thank you. Got the point. We need to go down about fifteen decks at least to have any access to the hanger bay. Bryan, you're anchor for the top. Alisa, you're the lightest. You'll go down first," Alec ordered.

"Not the first time you've asked me to go down.

Should have brought jetpacks," Alisa responded. She wrapped the rope around her waist and went down the tube. Bryan tied the other end to himself as he lowered her down. Bryan let out a grunt when he let go of the rope. He would've fallen into the shaft himself if the others didn't catch him. They saw he'd been shot in the torso. He gasped in pain and anger, "Just go!"

Alisa yanked on the rope signaling she'd made it. Tara and Duncan slid down the rope as they came under more fire. Jane and Alec fired back. Bryan got hit three more times in the torso. He gasped in pain as he rasped, "Go!"

Jane pulled on Alec's shoulder, "Come on!"

The two of them slid down. Alec looked up as he went down seeing Bryan getting hit several more times. He fell backwards into the shaft with the line still attached. Alec swung into the open door and cut the line off of Alisa just in time. "What the fuck?" She asked. Alec sighed, "He's dead..." He paused for a second sighing in grief, "... and if he was still tied to you, you'd be to. The hanger should be just down that passageway."

He pointed as several Alliance operatives popped out of the corners firing upon them. They leaped out of the way as the shots suddenly stopped. Tara snapped, "What are they waiting for?"

Jane told her, "For us to pop out again."

Alisa sighed as she pulled out her pistol duel wielding that and her SMG. Duncan told her, "Duel wielding isn't effective!"

"It looks bad ass! If I'm going out, I'm going out in a blaze of glory!" She spun around the corner going as fast as she could. The others provided as much cover fire as possible without hitting her. When her shields went out, she leaped up against the bulkhead right next to a soldier and shot him with the pistol while kneeing another in the face. As she went down digging her knee into the soldier's face mask crushing his head, she fired her SMG at another operative. She took a couple more hits as she slammed down on the deck. Alisa emptied her pistol round in the nearest soldier while pinning down the last two operatives. The others charged forward supporting her as she kept going. She started repeatedly jabbing her empty SMG into the face mask of one operative while shoving into another one. With blood coming out of the cracks of the mask, she shoved the dead body into the last soldier and went around stabbing him in the neck with a plasma knife killing him. She turned around laughing, "Hell fucking…!"

She got shot in the chest right where her heart was. Alisa dropped backwards as the other turned around seeing the same operative that had been stalking them go down the elevator shaft while leaving grenades rolling right at them. Duncan yelled, "Duck!"

The grenades went off knocking them all down. Duncan was screaming, "It burns!"

He took the brunt of the blast and was on his back with shards of shrapnel all over him. Alec ran over and started dragging him along, "You're going to be okay!"

"Shit!" He said as the same operative came out of the elevator shaft firing at them. He scored a hit on Duncan making him cry louder. Alec went as fast as he could and rounded a corner for cover. Tara and Jane kept firing pinning him down. Alec placed Duncan upright as his lower half suddenly got detached from his lower half again. He moaned in agony. Alec removed his helmet as he cried, "It's going to be okay!"

"Fucking shit... what was it all for?" He asked as he started gagging on his own blood. Alec said, "Liberty?"

"We've been turned to fucking alien whores. Everything we've been working for was lies. Fucking bullshit!" He moaned as his eyes started closing over and over again. Alec shook him, "Don't wuss out on me!"

"Get out of here. Tell my son... as bad as things get, he still has his dick attached... don't lose it." Duncan's eyes rolled up in the back of his head and blood gushed out of his mouth. Alec shed a tear, "No..."

Jane went over to him, "He's dead! We're almost out of here! We need to go!"

Alec slowly got up as Tara patted him on the shoulder, "We'll get laid! It'll make everything better."

Alec weakly laughed as Jane opened the hanger bay doors. She quickly went back pushing both Tara and Alec back as several rounds came through the door. They leaned against the bulkhead as the hits heated up from the round impacting on the other side. Jane looked back, "I got this one."

She went over to lob a grenade. As it left her hand, her arm got shot off. Jane let out a shrill scream as Tara pulled her back. It was the same operatives that had been stalking them. Alec saw a red spot on the bulkhead. He looked back, "Hold on."

He threw his last grenade at the spot hard enough where it went into the metal. The blast ripped open a hole wide enough for them to fit through. Tara went in first. They both looked at each other as Alec gave her a nod. She went through the hole and ran right up to a soldier. Before she could react, Tara shot her in the head, spun her around and used her as a shield. Jane and Alec went in next. Both of them held down their triggers enraged by their losses. The last three operatives went down in the hail storm. Tara snapped as she started to reload, "Assholes!"

Alec saw a Raven transport that was ready to launch. "You said something about getting laid?"

"I believe I did," she laughed as they went forward to join them. Another operative came up behind her. She managed to turn around and shoot him in the head multiple times causing him to drop. She ran out of ammo and laughed, "Almost..." She suddenly froze as a loud bang echoed in the hanger. Tara stumbled forward as Alec tried to go forward. Jane pulled him back as she screamed. It took her all the strength she had left to push him inside the transport. The lone operative armed with a sniper rifle went up to her and then looked up at both Alec and Jane. He yelled, "No!"

The Alliance operative shot Tara in the head. Things moved in slow motion for Alec as he saw her body slam onto the deck lifelessly. Jane cried, "Hold that asshole off! I'm taking this bird out!"

Alec enraged fired back at him as he went side to side dodging the rounds. The transport lifted into the air as it fired away at the doors, enough to blast though them. The suction of space sped up the launching of the Raven as it left the station. Before the engines could give the transport thrust, the Alliance operative came flying towards them. Alec tried closing the doors, but it was too late. The operative came into the ship, slamming into

Alec. He knocked Alec across the empty cargo compartment into the bulkhead. When he did, he kicked back against it flying at the operative. He fired and missed him as he was tackled by Alec. He lost his grip on his rifle while slapping the weapon out of Alec's hands. Both of them slammed back against the doors as the man punched Alec in the head. Alec then kicked him, sending the operative in the opposite direction. Alec grabbed his SMG. The operative aimed with his rifle. Both of them shot at each other, hitting the other's weapon. Alec went back against the door and pushed himself forward at the soldier who swung his rifle like a club and Alec in the head. Again he went flying into a bulkhead. He kicked against it flying at the soldier who didn't react fast enough as Alec started hitting him over and over again in the face mask. The operative kicked Alec off and kicked him again going for the cockpit. Alec saw him coming up behind Jane, "Look out!"

She spun around in her chair with a pistol aiming at the operative. He grabbed the weapon and moved the muzzle away from himself. Jane fired and miss him hitting a console behind them sending sparks flying in the compartment. She started kicking him over and over buying Alec enough time to rebound towards the cockpit. He pulled out his knife lunging it towards the soldier as he struggled with Jane's pistol. He saw him coming and aimed the pistol at Alec. The operative forced her to fire. The weapon went off hitting him in the shoulder. The man elbowed Jane in the head and reached for Alec's arm. The operative forced the knife into Jane's torso. She screamed as she got stabbed. Alec punched him in the head sending him face first into the controls.

Alec saw the Pandora's hanger bay get larger and larger as they came in for a crash landing. Emergency nets shot up from the deck as they came in. Despite being slowed down by them, they still slammed into the bulkhead, smashing the cockpit. The Alliance operative was the first one to get up and drift out of the broken door of the transport as sparks flew inside. Alec got up having a hard time moving. He went over to Jane seeing she died on impact. He growled as he grabbed her pistol. He kicked with his good leg flying towards the exit. As he exited the hanger, he saw outside the ship. The rest of the fleet was getting slaughtered by the Alliance armada. A group of Alliance's ships concentrated fire on a lone star shaped ship, destroying it in a single volley of torpedoes. In a single flash, a ship would vanish into a red, orange and yellow ball of flame sending shards of metal throughout space.

The Pandora seemed to be the only working ship,

as it was the only one firing back at the Alliance. It was retrieving as many fighters and transports as it could as it backed away from the fight. Alec never felt so helpless seeing everything he worked hard to build get destroyed mercilessly. He looked down at the operative as he turned around. Alec kicked the transport flying down at him with the pistol aimed at the operative. The soldier quickly pulled out his side arm and aimed, too. Both of them fired at the same time. Alec crashed into him sending both of them into a tumble across the hanger. When they bounced off against the bulkhead Alec felt he'd been hit in the chest. He grabbed his wound as he looked at the operative. He got hit in the face mask causing it to be ripped off. It was Marley's face. He was the Alliance operative that killed his team. Marley gasped for air trying to hold his mouth and nose shut. Alec gave him the finger. Both of them aimed their pistols at each other. In one single flash, it went dark.

CHAPTER 20
KILL YOSEMITE
UNKNOWN DATE
UNKNOWN SYSTEM
PANDORA
HANGER BAY

MARLEY opened his eyes, and he was back on the Pandora. The lights were flickering and the air was filled with smoke. He heard shouting, "Got some explaining to do jackass!"

He sat up seeing Doc and... Alec. He was in a new body and was holding Doc by the neck. The doctor smiled as he hit both of Alec's arms, breaking free. He kicked Alec in the chest sending him against the wall. Marley asked "What the hell is going on?"

Doc looked over at him with glowing blue eyes, "Change. I'll tell you more after you kill Yosemite."

Marley got up feeling he was still in an armored suit. The air seemed to smell of burnt meat and metal. He saw to his horror several burnt bodies around him, "What the fuck?"

"It was the pulse!" Alec snapped as he got up looking at Marley with rage in his eyes. "It was repurposed to kill sentient organisms! This asshole tampered with the programming! Oh, now that we aren't sharing the same body anymore, I'm going to repay you for killing me!"

He rushed forward at Marley with the doctor stopping him, "Did you not hear what I said? Kill Yosemite! This might be our only chance! You'll have a fair fight now that he's wounded."

"What?" Both of them asked in confusion. Doc pointed Alec towards his armored suit and sighed, "Didn't want to do this, but now's not the time to drag heels. As your maker, will you two go kill Yosemite?"

Marley suddenly felt compelled to kill Yosemite. It was like killing him would scratch a burning itch that he suddenly felt. Alec tensed up for a second before he walked into the suit and got armored up. Once he moved around inside of it, Alec sighed, "Let's go."

They both grabbed plasma shotguns and pistols before heading out. Doc smiled as they walked down the passageway. Nothing seemed to matter to them, but killing Yosemite. Both of them started to run forward leaping over the dead. They didn't seem to matter to them right now. Must kill Yosemite. There was a red dot flashing on their head up display showing them where they'd find him. The closer the dot got to them the more they felt urgency to get there. Both of them were at a dead sprint going as fast as they could. It appeared Yosemite was heading to the hanger bay. "He's not getting away!" Marley snapped. Both of them rushed through the doors leading to the bay. Marley saw several hundred dead on the flight deck between the fighters and drop ships, all of them frozen in their last moments of agony with their hands reaching up to their heads. Steam was still rising from the ruptures in their suits. For once he wasn't shocked. He didn't seem to care. Have to kill Yosemite. Marley lifted his rifle into the air and swept the room with the muzzle looking for his target. Alec covered the opposite section. The lights went out leaving them in the dark. Their night vision came up showing green images. Suddenly, several shots rang out in the air. Marley spun around seeing Alec firing up at the catwalks above then a loud thud down below.

"Did you really think I'd be that easy to kill?" Yosemite's voice echoed in the massive room. Both of them slowly moved forward taking care not to make a sound with their suits. They listened for the direction of the voice. Yosemite's speech was like needles in their ears. The two drop ships in front of them gave Yosemite just enough room to hide. "He must be over there," thought

Alec. He went right, and Marley went left. Both kept eyes up above. Something swiped at Marley's legs. He leaped back firing at the deck as Yosemite rolled away from the rounds. There was an explosion and Alec went flying backwards using his suit's boosters to escape the blast.

From above, several flash bang grenades went off. Marley turned around to avoid being blinded while ducking behind some crates. A grenade suddenly landed in front of him. He rolled over the crates with Yosemite firing away. He moved out of the way with my shields taking a couple hits. The explosives went off sending the crates flying in the air. Marley launched up into the air throwing grenades at Yosemite's direction. Alec was taking pot shots at him. Yosemite managed to shoot the grenades while they were still in midair sending Marley flying into the ground. Alec had his shotgun blasted out from his hands as Yosemite leaped over to him and knocked him down with a kick to his head. Marley fired. Yosemite ducked into a ball, and his shield deflected all the rounds. He went backwards as Alec fired at him with his side arm. Yosemite left a couple grenades for him. Alec leaped into a nearby fighter avoiding the blast. The impact caused the fighter to flip over. Alec was stuck inside. Marley got back up seeing Yosemite standing above him on a drop ship. He was almost naked with burn marks and shriveled up skin all over his body. His teeth were worn and cracked and looked pained. Three of his four eyes were gone, and his limbs looked like they were being held together by a few shards of metal. "Just you and me now machine!"

Marley quickly fired up at him as he leaped up into the air and landed behind him. He lunged at him with a plasma dagger. Marley leaned away and swiped with his shotgun causing him to miss. With his free arm, Yosemite pointed a pistol at Marley's head. He moved forward, dodging the round as it passed by his head. Yosemite kicked at him with both of his feet at his stomach. Marley used his knees to block and went flying backwards into a drop ship so hard it left a dent.

Yosemite was about to shoot Marley as he tried to break free when he came under fire from three others. It was Yeager, Jane and Kathryn. They handed Alec and Marley new rifles. Yosemite barely managed to stay away from the rounds as they flew past him and impacted his shields. The fighter that Alec was stuck in suddenly came flying forward at Yosemite. He managed to leap over it as the Hawk crashed against the bulkhead. Yosemite landed on his feet while grunting. He was showing signs of wear and tear. Yosemite started laughing, "Not cheating and not trying? Never thought I would die by those words."

He rushed forward as everyone all fired at him.

Turns out it was a holo-image of him. He leaped clear over everyone and landed in front of a doorway as it closed in front of him. He laughed again as he dropped another flash bang grenade, "Should have tried to take down the ship instead of escaping."

He vanished when it went off. All of them formed a loose circle looking around for him. "Should have just cut my losses instead of trying to keep the fight going," muttered Yosemite.

One of the drop ships came to life and opened fire at the team with plasma rounds. They all scattered as Yeager fired back with a rocket. The drop ship went down like a brick with the front end twisted and burnt. Yosemite landed right in front of Yeager, cutting his hands off and kicking him down. He bent backward repeatedly shooting Alec in the arms and legs. Yosemite spun sideways and again disappeared behind a fighter. Alec was down on the deck screaming, "Get him!"

"I should never have trusted that alien. I let my own augmentation cloud my judgment," Jane sighed as she was suddenly pinned between a fighter and a bulkhead. Two rockets came flying from the fighter. Marley ducked down, dodging one of them as it came flying overhead. The second one ripped Kathryn's legs off as it went into her. Both rockets impacted into the door, blasting it open. "At least I'm glad I got those upgrades," remarked Kathryn.

Yosemite started running to the door. Marley didn't shoot at the image he saw. He wouldn't fall for the hologram a second time. Instead Marley looked over and saw Yosemite running up along the bulkhead for the other door. Marley fired a grenade at where he'd be. It landed right in between his legs and sent him flying into the air. His legs bent in unnatural directions. Yosemite landed near Marley screaming and holding his groin, "You unethical genital shooter!"

"Killing you should make things better." Marley said. He didn't feel bad about killing the alien. He normally would. This time, Marley just wanted him dead. Yosemite laughed, "Still a puppet. Just different set of strings pulling you now."

Marley fired at him with a few rounds hitting their mark. Yosemite's shield absorbed the rounds long enough for him to get close to Marley, cutting his rifle in half. Marley quickly pulled out his knife and used it to block the attacks. He waited for an opening as Yosemite kept swiping at him. Marley then went for the limbs and stabbed him in the kneecap. Yosemite let out a scream and hit Marley in the head hard enough to knock his helmet off. Yosemite pulled the knife out and threw it at Marley who rolled out of the way as it stabbed into the deck.

Yosemite yelled, "I should have let you die!"

"Should have, could have, too late now," Marley said as Yosemite stabbed at him again. Marley managed to dodge the blade, get his knife back and cut one of Yosemite's arms off. He kicked Marley in the chest, sending him flat against the deck. He threw another grenade at Marley as he darted for the door. Marley leaped forward cutting the grenade in half before it exploded. The two halves exploded behind Marley as more grenades were dropped. He went flying in the air avoiding the blast. Marley pulled out a pistol and fired. He landed a hit before Yosemite got into the passageway. The shot landed in the same leg that was just stabbed. Marley couldn't believe Yosemite was still going after taking so many injures. Why couldn't he just die?

Marley chased after Yosemite down the passageway as he quickly limped away from him. He managed to keep ducking behind a bulkhead. There was no clear shot for Marley to take, but he had to try. Marley went around the corner firing anyway, seeing nothing but empty corridors. Then, he saw a shadow move behind him. Marley flipped around as Yosemite tried to attach a grenade to him and kick him away. Instead, Marley knocked his arm out of the way, causing him to miss. The grenade went off, sending them both down the passageway. They punched each other as they flew. Blood, sparks and steam came from Yosemite's empty eye sockets and wounds. With each punch Yosemite's bones bucked under the strain. His jaw was ripped in half with metal bones sticking out and sparks dropping. Both of them struggled to get back up. Yosemite yelled, "Damned machine!"

He pulled a second dagger from his belt and lunged at Marley one more time. Marley dodged his attack and cut his other arm off. He cried again. Yosemite didn't stop. He leaped forward and wrapped his legs around Marley while putting the last grenade into his mouth. If Yosemite wasn't going to make it out alive, Marley wasn't either. Frantically, Marley punched him as hard as he could, snapping his neck before the grenade went off. As Yosemite's body vaporized, Marley went flying into a bulkhead with his armor falling apart. He started laughing as blue liquid came flowing out of his broken body. Marley was happy. Yosemite was dead this time. He felt a release before everything went black.

CHAPTER 21
ALIVE
DATE UNKNOWN
PANDORA
INFIRMARY

MARLEY open his eyes and started to laugh with joy. He might have been sick of the infirmary, but he was fine with being there this time, as long as Yosemite was dead now. Yosemite is dead! He didn't think he'd get so much thrill from killing someone, but he was happy about what he did. Doc came up to him, "Well done, Mr. Marley."

"Thank you. Wait… what?" He was confused. He started to think again. Marley wasn't being driven by instinct anymore. He looked up at Doc, "What the hell is going on? Why is most of the crew dead?"

"Don't worry. We can bring most of them back, worked with you and Alec."

"What?" He asked sitting up and looking over to his right. He gasped when he saw himself, but dead.

Marley leaped off the bed and moved against the bulkhead, "What the hell?!"

He explained, "I can take people's electrical impulses from their brains and transfer that from one body to another, kind of like switching hard drives with computers."

Marley looked down at the dead body asking, "Wait, so I'm just a copy then? I'm not the real Calvin Marley? Who am I? What am I?"

"Ever heard of Theseus Ship?" Doc asked. Marley replied, "Heard of the man, but not the ship."

Doc explained, "The ship that Theseus uses has just about everything switched out and replaced during its journey. By the time it comes back, almost nothing remains of the original. It's not the same ship. I live with it because I believe as long as that vessel carries out its mission and has the spirit of the vessel it's named after, it's really still the same. Fight for the cause you believe in, and you'll be just as much the person you think yourself to be."

"You said something to me that really spurred me on earlier. How can I have a cause if I've been a puppet this whole time?" Marley asked looking him in his artificial eyes. He was blunt, "You want humanity to be free right?"

"Yes."

"Then you have a cause. If you want to restore

humanity, keep your convictions," Doc told him. "What did we do to humanity?" Marley asked.

"Like I said, I was able to make copies. This ship had enough room for everyone. The only problem is that currently they are disembodied and in digital form." he told him. Marley snapped, "How does that help humanity?"

"If my experiment worked properly, no one will have lost their bodies at all," he told him. Marley wondered, "What's that supposed to mean?"

"If space can be manipulated for galactic travel, then why not just manipulate time to do the same?" he proposed. Marley looked confused again, "Time travel?"

Doc nodded, "Tell me what you see the next time you pass out."

"I just woke up! I'm done resting," Marley got up and started walking toward the airlock. "Fair warning, you'll be bumping into ghost," he hinted.

"Fuck off!" Marley said to him as he slammed the door to the airlock. He started to make his way to the mess decks ready to have a drink of any kind. He went through the doors and saw the others sitting around talking. They paused their conversation as Marley walked in, "What?"

Alec turned around smiling as he ripped out a table from its foundation and threw it at Marley's head before he could react. Marley was out in an instant.

EPILOGUE

MARLEY opened his eyes and saw a woman standing in front of him. She looked a lot like Doc, or at least like she was in the same family group. He was having a hard time adjusting his eyes. "What year is it?" the woman asked him.

Marley thought about it for a second, "2212 the last time I checked."

"Hmm…interesting. What if I told you that time is not linear?" She asked him while shutting down her holo-monitor and looking over at him with anticipation. Marley replied, "I'd say you know something I don't. That or maybe I can travel through time?"

She smiled, "I know a lot more than you ever will. So going off of the current information you have, do you like how things are turning out?"

"No! Our system is dead. Both groups of aliens are now going to be hot on our heels! If this isn't a lousy situation, I don't know what is."

"I have. I survived. That's what we do best. So you'd change things if you could?" She asked him while giving him a look of excitement. "Yes," he replied, "I'd try to make things better."

"Effort is what matters most. Anything can happen with the right amount of it," she said with glee. He looked at her puzzled, "Are you related to Doc?"

"In a manner of speaking," she told him. He nodded, "I'll take that as a yes. He's also very vague. So do you know of a way things can change?"

"They already have. Why do you think you're at the Slip Gate again?"

"To try again?" he replied slowly while shrugging. His vision got better, and he saw he was back in the infirmary. The room looked the same, but something seemed off. "Did Doc mention time travel?" she asked.

"Yes. I'm guessing it worked, right?"

"That it did!" she told him while grabbing a rifle from behind her desk. "Here is how it works…"

She clubbed him across the head hard enough to knock him out of his chair. He went flat on his back with a concussion. She knelt down next to him, "Change what you can, while you can."